Vms

KT-520-865

RIPENING VINE

A frantic SOS from her friend Kerry sends Rose rushing to France to see if she can help. In the Dordogne, Kerry's problems are resolved—but Rose is confronted with problems herself, problems that are not of her own making. She meets the local lord of the manor, Philippe du Caine—a man who was not of her world any more than she was of his. Any involvement with him will only lead to heartbreak—but how can she get away?

RIPENING VINE

ARNOLDFIELD COURT

Ripening Vine

by

Ellen Clare

Magna Large Print Books

Long Preston, North Yorkshire,
England.

British Library Cataloguing in Publication Data.

Clare, Ellen
 Ripening vine.

 A catalogue record for this book is
 available from the British Library

ISBN 0-7505-0886-8

First published in Great Britain by Mills & Boon Ltd.,
1981

Copyright © 1981 by Ellen Clare

Published in Large Print July 1995 by arrangement with
Harlequin Enterprises, B.V., Switzerland.

All rights reserved. No part of this publication may be
reproduced, stored in a retrieval system, or transmitted in any
form or by any means, electronic, mechanical, photocopying,
recording or otherwise, without the prior permission of the
Copyright owner.

LINCOLNSHIRE
COUNTY COUNCIL

Magna Large Print is an imprint of
Library Magna Books Ltd.
Printed and bound in Great Britain by
T.J. Press (Padstow) Ltd., Cornwall, PL28 8RW.

All the characters in this book have no existence outside the imagination of the Author, and have no relation whatsoever to anyone bearing the same name or names. They are not even distantly inspired by any individual known or unknown to the Author, and all the incidents are pure invention.

CHAPTER ONE

Rose Robinson drove southwards through France, her little green Mini purred along the undulating, winding road beyond the valley of the Dordogne. On either side of her vineyards and fields of maize stretched across the sunlit countryside, ripening in the heat. Rose, who looked as English as her name, was eighteen and a half and she had left school only a month ago after taking her 'A' levels. The results were yet to be announced, but it wasn't that which worried her at that moment.

She was a tall girl with fair wavy hair, gentle features and a soft petal-smooth skin that glowed with healthy youthfulness. Her figure was a little too rounded to be willowy, but she carried herself well and the light cotton dress she had made for herself fitted neatly and modestly, enhancing but certainly not flaunting her essential femininity.

Yesterday morning she had driven the two hundred miles from her home town in Norfolk, England, had crossed the Channel by ferryboat in the early afternoon and last night had stayed at a small tourist hotel—L'Hôtel des Voyageurs—overlooking a central square where beneath shady trees on a long sandy pitch, men played at *boules* until darkness fell.

She would have really enjoyed the trip if it had not been for that nagging worry about Kerry. What was it that had upset her friend so much? Rose remembered vividly the distress in Kerry's voice when she had telephoned her at home just a few evenings ago. It had been almost eleven o'clock on a warm summer evening, Rose had been sitting quietly at home with her parents, when the phone rang with that fateful message.

'Hello—'

'Rose? Oh, thank goodness I've got through to you!'

'Kerry! How lovely to hear from you. I thought you'd be in France—'

'I am. I'm in a public callbox in Chandelle. I don't know how much time I've got and I've already lost ten francs on a wrong number.'

'Okay, fire away. I'm listening.'

'Rose, are you terribly busy? I—I mean,

have you arranged to go away or anything?'

'No plans exactly. I told you when I wrote, I'm looking for a temporary job—'

'Yes, that's what I was banking on. Rose, could you come out and stay with me? I'm at the Villa.'

'I'd love to—perhaps in a couple of weeks—'

'No, I mean now. As soon as you can. Please, Rose—I need someone to talk to.'

'What's the matter, Kerry? Are you all right?'

'Yes, at least, more or less.' She sounded dispirited, not at all the cheerful girl she usually was. 'I can't tell you over the phone, but I'll go mad if I stay here alone.'

'Aren't your parents there?'

'They've gone home. They left yesterday. We had the most awful row, but I just couldn't go back with them and finally they agreed to let me stay on here—but it's horrible on my own. Oh, Rose, do say you'll come and stay with me. It's—it's lovely here really—I mean, the countryside and all that. Will you—please, Rose?'

'Well, yes, all right, Kerry. I'll see—'

Kerry had given her no chance for further equivocation.

'Thank you—thank you! You're a real pal. You don't know what a relief that is—'

The telephone had buzzed warningly.

'Come as soon as you can. I'll be looking out. You know the address?'

'Yes. I think—'

There had been no more time for words. The line had gone dead. Rose had never had any doubts that she must go to France in answer to Kerry's call. The two girls had been close friends, almost like sisters, until two years ago when Kerry's family had moved away to Bournemouth. Mr Langham had been promoted by his firm, financially he had become much better off than were the Robinsons, but that had made no difference to Kerry and Rose. Last summer Rose had stayed with the Langhams in their new home, for three glorious weeks and she and Kerry had had such fun.

Then Kerry and her parents had gone to their holiday villa in Southern France. She had written to Rose afterwards, telling her about this smashing young Frenchman she had met and how they had spent almost every day together, swimming, playing tennis, walking, driving in his little sports car. It had sounded idyllic, and Rose had been envious—now she was not so sure. This year something had evidently gone wrong. She could still hear the note of desperation in Kerry's voice, a little choked sob of a sound—something serious had happened to Kerry, of that she felt sure.

It had not been easy for Rose to persuade her parents that she would be perfectly capable of driving through France on her own to stay with Kerry. However, they were beginning to come to terms with the fact that their only daughter was a child no longer, that physically and legally she was now a woman, though that did not alter their deeply protective attitude towards her. Rose accepted their love and concern with gratitude, but at the same time, she knew she must sometimes make a stand for independence—and this was one of those times.

So here she was, already well south on the journey. She glanced at her watch. It was half past four. She calculated that she had at least another hour's driving to get to Chandelle. She pressed her foot harder on the accelerator, and the car responded though it had seldom been driven so fast.

The little green Mini was a great luxury. It was seven years old but had been carefully looked after, having belonged to Rose's grandmother who had given it to her about six months previously.

'I know you'll drive it sensibly and not take any silly risks,' she had said fondly, handing the keys to Rose.

'Oh, Gran, you're so good to me,' Rose had said, throwing her arms around the old lady. 'But I wish—I wish you could still drive it yourself.'

'Nothing anyone can do about that.' Her grandmother had glanced down at her hands, twisted with arthritis. 'I can't drive any more, but I've still got a lot to be thankful for.'

'I'll come and take you out whenever you want,' said Rose.

She had done just that as often as possible. Gran lived only a few streets away from them, but just now she was away in Australia, spending three months' holiday with her younger son, who had emigrated several years ago. Gran had been a slow and careful driver and Rose herself was usually quite happy to keep to moderate speeds, mindful of her promise to be careful. Now she began to feel a mounting sense of urgency. Kerry's voice, the slight break that was almost a sob, kept recurring in her mind. It stirred a fear that something terrible might happen to her friend if she remained too long alone.

It was then Rose noticed the warning light glowing red on the dashboard. Automatically she lifted her foot off the accelerator; and the car slowed. There were no other indications that anything was amiss, no splutterings from the engine, no loss of power—what was it that the warning light indicated?

Rose had never encountered it before in the short time she had been driving. She was in the midst of a vast plain; open countryside stretched all around her. If she stopped there was nothing she could do—she would not know how to mend whatever it was that was wrong with the car. There was little traffic about, and even if there had been Rose would have hesitated to flag down another car in the hope of enlisting help. She would have been reluctant to do that even in England, but here in a foreign land it was unthinkable. The nervous tension she had been building up in her mind about Kerry began to transmit itself to her own person, making her feel vulnerable. As long as the car kept going she decided to carry on and to stop at the next garage.

Surely there would be a village soon? She drove more slowly; that must be the sensible thing to do. Anxiously she glanced at the red warning light, hoping against hope that it had been some mere freak, that it would switch itself off, that all would yet be well. It remained like an insistent, unblinking eye staring at her, mocking her ignorance. If only she had brought the car manual, she could have looked to see what the trouble was, though even if she knew, it was doubtful whether she could have done anything about it.

The road stretched interminably ahead and the heat danced, making a mirage of the distance—surely soon there would be a village, a wayside garage? She carried on and on and at last saw a line of poplar trees a mile or so ahead. To her relief she saw the sign *Les Virages. Visitez l'église du XVIème siècle, le musée, le pont du Moyen-Age.* It was an old and historic town.

Slowly she drove through the avenue of poplars which led into a narrow street where tall houses of grey stone closed in tight on either side. The place thronged

16

with people. Narrow though the pavements were, space had been found to set small tables and chairs outside the cafés; groups of elderly black-clad women and white-haired men wearing the traditional berets stood chatting; tourists wandered in shorts and sun-dresses; a child darted across the road with a bundle of long crusty *baguettes* clasped in his arms. The very Frenchness of it would have delighted Rose, if she had not been so worried about the car.

Not only was the red warning light glowing but she was now aware that the temperature gauge was pointing to hot. At last she saw a garage. Thankfully she drove on to the forecourt and stopped a couple of yards behind a powerful sports car, very dark blue in colour, which was being filled with petrol. Rose stepped out and was horrified. Steam rose from the bonnet of her Mini. The car was boiling. The pump attendant looked up, so amazed that he jerked the nozzle and spilled some petrol.

Two mechanics in oil-stained dungarees looked up from their work. *'Mon Dieu!'* exclaimed one, the other gave an astonished whistle. Interest was centred with almost equal intensity on Rose and on the state

17

of her car, by now almost lost in a cloud of steam. One man laughed, the sort of incredulous, spontaneous laughter that greets the fool who steps on a banana skin in a slapstick comedy. Rose felt ridiculous as well as concerned.

With a leisurely swagger both mechanics walked over to the car. One put his hand on the bonnet, as if to open it, but it was too hot to handle. He drew in his breath between his teeth and shook his head. They were talking in a quick *patois* that was incomprehensible to Rose, though French had been one of her main subjects at school. She bit her lip and looked at them helplessly.

'Qu'est-ce que c'est?' she asked.

The answer came with a flood of technical jargon that she had no hope of understanding. The petrol pump attendant had finished serving his customer, who now got out of his car. They both walked across to where Rose stood beside her steaming Mini. It seemed to her that everybody in the town would soon know about her misfortune. A knot of small boys appeared as if by magic and all seemed to be vociferously and hilariously discussing Rose and her car. A puddle of water trickled from beneath it—it was the final humiliation.

'*Mademoiselle,* did you not see the red warning light?'

That question came in English, with the merest trace of an accent overlying its resonance. It was the man from the powerful sports car.

'Yes, but—'

She floundered. He was very tall and as he looked down at her she became aware of his deep dark eyes, the colour of bitter chocolate, lit with highlights. She met his stare as calmly as she could and those eyes opened wide, flickered over her in a rapid assessment that made her feel more foolish than ever. She was sure he thought her utterly incompetent, yet at the same time she read in his expression an indefinable interest that was typically—even aggressively masculine. She reacted to the confrontation with embarrassment—the more so as she felt an immediate quickening of her pulse, a sensation that made her angry with herself. It was only with a deliberate effort that she kept her cool.

'When the warning light shines, it is to tell you something is wrong and you must stop immediately.'

There was a note of condescension in his voice that roused resentment in her—it was so very male!

'I did stop as soon as possible—this is the first garage I've come across since that light came on. It wouldn't have been sensible to stop out there in the middle of nowhere, would it?'

'It would have been better than to land yourself in this trouble. France is a civilised country. Someone would have brought a message to the garage and they would have sent help.'

'I prefer to be independent.'

A mocking smile lifted one corner of his lips. 'An unwise aspiration, *mademoiselle*, unless you happen to be a skilled mechanic.'

She hated the continued criticism, the more so since probably she deserved it, and in the way he was looking at her there was an expression that somehow suggested she was nothing but a silly girl-child. Her response was antagonistic—she refused to play the part of helpless female which he seemed to have allotted her and which no doubt would have flattered his masculine ego. She tossed her head.

'Do you own this garage?' she asked.

'No.'

'Then since I got here with no inconvenience to myself or anyone else, I'm sure I can now leave it to the professionals to mend the car for me.'

His eyes hardened. 'I take it your French is also sufficient for you to understand the exact nature of the problem with your car?'

Rose had no chance to find out because the mechanic, who evidently knew this big, overbearing and interfering chauvinist well, turned to him to explain the problem. She tried to follow what they were saying as the man fired one or two questions, but from the shrug he received in reply as well as the few words she could sort out from the rapid technical conversation, she gathered she would be unable to drive any farther that day—and maybe not the next either.

She began to concentrate less on what they were saying and more on the man himself. His hair was a brown so dark that in less bright sunlight it would surely be taken for black and it swept back in waves which sprang into place when he ran an impatient hand through them. His features were clear-cut, the nose arrogantly aquiline with a slight scar on the bridge which, far from marring his handsome face, added character. There was no weakness in the firm mouth and the chin jutted with a hint of stubbornness. His whole attitude was that of a man used to taking command and of having his orders obeyed—well, if he expected subservience from her he would be disappointed, she decided. But even as she watched and listened some of the rebelliousness in her faded. She felt more and more helpless—she had no alternative but to acknowledge that she could not cope with this situation alone. The man turned to her, one eyebrow lifted quizzically.

'Did you understand that?'

Rose shook her head.

'Then may I interpret?'

'Yes, please.'

'The fan belt broke, making the engine overheat, then the radiator boiled dry and the result is you have ruined your head-gasket. It won't be possible to repair it this evening—in any case the garage will soon be closing. They don't carry the necessary spares, so it may be a day or two before they can fix it.'

Rose's heart sank lower and lower. Her dismay must have shown in her face, for he then asked, with rather more sympathy than before, 'Have you far to go, *mademoiselle?*'

'I—I'm not sure. I'm on my way to Chandelle—'

'Chandelle? That's not far, I'll take you—'

'Oh, no, *monsieur,* I wouldn't dream of troubling you.'

No doubt he expected her to welcome his offer. It seemed to Rose that he must be well aware of his attractiveness to women, but that made her all the more determined to resist. She drew away from him literally as well as figuratively and sensed rather than saw the flash of those deep, dark eyes. A hesitation crept into her voice, making it sound stilted and unnatural.

'Surely there will—be a—a bus or—or a train—'

He turned to the mechanic and spoke in French. 'Is there a bus or a train, Monsieur Brun?'

Monsieur Brun consulted the petrol pump attendant. Both men shook their heads. There was no public transport.

'There are hotels,' suggested Monsieur Brun, pointing into the town. 'No doubt Mademoiselle can be accommodated there for two or three nights until her car is ready.'

Come as soon as you can—Kerry's plea sounded in her ears yet again. She had to get to Chandelle tonight, even if she had to swallow her pride to do so. The stranger was watching her so closely that his eyes seemed to stare into her very soul—though it was an entirely physical reaction to his expression that made her cheeks flame. She was cross with herself and felt foolish for having refused his simple sensible offer so precipitately. Suddenly he seemed to take pity on her discomfiture. His face broke into a wide smile that made him seem much more human.

'But of course—we have not been properly introduced. Monsieur Brun, please be so good as to tell the young lady my name.'

'Why, *monsieur,* everybody knows you,' Monsieur Brun laughed. 'Monsieur du Caine from the Château Chandelle.'

'You mean you're going to Chandelle, too?'

'As I would have mentioned if you had not been so quick to refuse my offer,' he said with a wry smile.

'I'm—I'm so sorry.'

'And your name?'

Rose held out her hand with a conciliatory smile. 'I'm Rose Robinson.'

His handshake was warm, the pressure of his fingers gentle but firm.

'Rose Robinson.'

He repeated the name as if he intended to remember it. His accent was then slightly more pronounced, giving added resonance to the initial letters, speaking them from deep in his throat. He made it sound quite special—until then she had thought it so mundane as to be almost comical.

'Perhaps you will allow me the pleasure of giving you a lift?'

'Yes, please, Monsieur du Caine.'

In minutes her luggage was transferred to his car and Monsieur du Caine held open the door, she slid into the low but comfortable passenger seat, there was a pleasant smell of leather from the upholstery. Soon he was driving away from Les Virages, out to the open road and the car gathered speed. As she would have expected, he handled the car with precision. She didn't like Monsieur du Caine, and she never would, Rose decided, but in his arrogant way he had been helpful so she felt an obligation to make polite conversation.

'How lovely it is here with this glorious sunshine—is it always as nice as this?'

'Through most of the summer,' he replied easily. 'Is this your first visit to France, *mademoiselle*?'

She told him of the school trip she had made last year. It had been to Paris, a city he knew well, and she found it was unexpectedly easy to talk to him; she even made him laugh as she described some of their schoolgirl adventures. She didn't care now if she sounded young and silly. Soon she would get out of his car and more likely than not would never see him again. Half an hour later they arrived at Chandelle, he slowed and the car rolled gently through the narrow cobbled streets.

'Where are you staying?' he asked.

'It's called the Villa Ste Thérèse. I'm afraid that's all I know.'

'I believe it's near the church. Chandelle is only a small village.'

They crossed a hump-backed bridge that spanned the river, then took a left-hand fork. Rose saw the Château then, grey stone walls rising from a slight eminence, and remembered that Monsieur Brun had introduced this man as Monsieur du Caine of the Château Chandelle. If that was his home it looked impressively grand, dominating the village. Before she could make any remark about it he had stopped the car outside a white-painted chalet, the name *Ste Thérèse* was fashioned in wrought iron beside the door.

'I believe this is it.' He got out of the car and walked round to open the door for her. 'Better see if there's anyone at home.'

Rose stepped quickly up a short flight of steps that led to a grassed front garden; more steps took her to the front door. Before she reached it, it was flung wide and Kerry rushed out.

'Rose! Oh, Rose, thank goodness you've got here!'

At once Rose was swept into a warm embrace, Kerry's cheek brushed affectionately against her, they hugged each other in spontaneous joy at their reunion. Then Rose extricated herself, aware that Monsieur du Caine had followed her, carrying her suitcase.

'Monsieur du Caine was kind enough to give me a lift after I had some trouble with my car,' she explained quickly. 'Have you met my friend Kerry Langham?'

'I haven't yet had that pleasure,' said Monsieur du Caine. He shook hands with Kerry, then set down the suitcase in the doorway. 'Now that I know you're safe, I'll get on my way.'

'Thank you very much for the lift—and for all your help,' Rose said. She held out her hand politely. 'Goodbye, Monsieur du Caine.'

'*Au revoir*, Rose Robinson,' he replied.

With long athletic strides he moved back to his car. Kerry's eyes were round with wonder.

'How did you come to meet up with him?'

Briefly Rose explained. They went into the house and Kerry showed her round. In the front there was a comfortable living-room and a well equipped kitchen, both with wide views across meadowland that led to where a river meandered. Later Rose knew she would enjoy exploring the village and the countryside, undoubtedly it was beautiful, but more immediately she had to find out what was the matter with Kerry.

'Let's have some coffee, then we can talk,' said Kerry. 'You don't know how

28

grateful I am to see you, Rose. I really thought I'd go out of my mind. I haven't been feeling well and then I began to get sorry for myself.'

The coffee was soon made and the girls sat one each side of the pinewood kitchen table. Rose looked at her friend. Kerry's face was pinched rather than pale and her lightly tanned skin lacked its usual lustre.

'What's the matter, Kerry?' Rose asked.

Kerry set down her coffee cup. She looked directly into Rose's eyes as if determined to face her whatever her reaction might be.

'I'm going to have a baby.'

The announcement left Rose stunned. She did not know how to respond, remembering how she and Kerry had both felt so strongly that sex before marriage was wrong. She still fervently believed that. A clock on the wall ticked loudly. She gathered herself together.

'Do you want to tell me any more about it, Kerry?' she asked gently.

Kerry reached across the table and grasped Rose's hands. 'Oh, you are a brick! I just worry myself sick when I'm here alone. I'll be able to cope, now you're here. My parents are furious—well, you can't blame them really, I suppose.'

Rose nodded understandingly.

'You remember I told you about Jacques?'

Again Rose nodded. She wasn't surprised to learn that he was the father.

'He's away doing his National Service now,' said Kerry.

'Does he know? About the baby, I mean?'

'He does now. I wasn't sure myself until last week—then I wrote and told him. I haven't heard from him since.'

Kerry's voice sounded small, that note of desperation crept into it again. Rose pressed the hand that was still curled inside hers.

'I expect you'll hear soon. Letters are slow sometimes and you're not on the telephone here, are you?'

'That's what I keep telling myself. But I do wish he'd get in touch with me.'

'He may not have been able to—perhaps his unit is on training exercises or something.'

Kerry's face brightened at the suggestion.

'Anyway,' Rose went on, 'how are you feeling in yourself?'

'Better, now you're here,' Kerry made

an effort at a smile. 'But I don't intend to lumber you with my troubles. Did you have a good journey?'

'I did until my car broke down.'

'And then you met up with our local lady-killer—the most sought-after bachelor in the district,' Kerry grinned. 'Did he make any advances to you, Rose?'

'I thought he was abominably overbearing. I'd have taken the bus from Les Virages if there had been one.'

'Ah, Les Virages!' Kerry said knowingly. 'That figures. Jacques says the great Philippe keeps one of his mistresses there.'

Rose raised an eyebrow. '*One* of his mistresses?'

Kerry giggled. 'That was how Jacques put it. And I've certainly seen his photograph in the papers with more than one glamorous female. There are plenty of women who would give their eye-teeth to marry Philippe du Caine, I can tell you. And I bet you never even made an effort to be sweet to him, Rose Robinson!'

Rose laughed. 'Absolutely true. In fact I believe I was really quite rude to him.'

'I'm glad at least you thanked him nicely before he left—Jacques' father is manager of the du Caines' estate and he's a bit feudal in his attitude to the family—Jacques' father is, I mean.'

'I promise to curtsey in my most subservient manner if we ever meet again,' Rose grinned.

'Just see that you do—at least till after Jacques and I are safely married,' said Kerry.

She was laughing, of course, but there was an undercurrent of seriousness. Anyway, Rose decided she was unlikely to have any more close contact with Philippe du Caine. With so many beautiful girls to choose from, Rose guessed he would scarcely remember her—and she was content that it should be so.

CHAPTER TWO

'I thought you'd like this room, because it's got such a lovely view,' said Kerry, leading the way upstairs.

Rose went to the window. Below her lay the garden of Ste Thérèse, sloping down to the road. The house had been built on a hill, a piece of which had been levelled out to make space for it. All around were lines of grapevines, thickly leaved, their bunches of almost ripe fruit hanging half hidden by the luxuriant foliage. They were trained and twisted to make picking and cultivation easy.

'Is it nearly time for the grape harvest?' asked Rose.

'Not yet, but I don't know much about it. Just about all the land here belongs to the du Caines. Shall I help you unpack?'

Rose's few dresses were soon hung in the big wardrobe. All the furniture was rather old-fashioned, a wide bed with a wooden head and foot, the wardrobe and chest of drawers in the same dark, heavy oak. The floor was of polished wood, with scattered rugs, shaggy sheepskins on either side. There were shutters to the window and it had a pleasant air of old-fashioned comfort in French country style.

'We bought the place furnished,' Kerry explained. 'Mum keeps saying we must change some of this furniture, but we haven't got around to doing it yet.'

'It's charming,' Rose murmured.

'I think it's hideous,' Kerry replied. 'But we have got new curtains and covers—the

33

old ones were so awful you wouldn't believe it. What shall we do about supper? Would you like to go to the café in the village or shall we make something here? I've got plenty of food in because I wasn't sure what time you would arrive.'

'I'd just as soon stay in tonight,' said Rose.

Together they prepared a simple supper —soup quickly made from a packet, cold meats and cheese with tomatoes, cucumber and dishes of ready-made Waldorf salad and coleslaw bought from the village delicatessen. The butter was fresh and creamy and the bread locally baked in long sticks mouth-meltingly light within a crisp crust.

'Mmmm! I love French bread,' Rose murmured, tearing off a length and spreading it thickly with butter.

'All local produce tonight,' Kerry laughed. 'Bread, butter, tomatoes, even the meats are from the local butcher, pâté from the shop.' She seemed as if she would never stop talking. 'Shall we make tea, or would you like to sample the local wine?'

'Tea for me, please,' said Rose.

Kerry picked up a tall green bottle and pointed to the label with a picture of a chateau on a scroll of paper yellowed to appear old, a border of vine leaves and the words *appellation contrôlée*. *Château Chandelle 1978*. Rose did not want to be so fascinated, but she found herself staring at the picture of the castle with its turrets, conical-topped, long lancet windows and narrow portico.

'Does the Château really look like that?' she asked.

Kerry looked at the picture. 'I've never really studied it before. Yes, I believe it must be an artist's impression of the real place, but he's made it rather taller and thinner looking. It's very grand and spacious—we'll go up there and see it when Jacques comes home.'

There was that break in her voice again as she spoke and Rose went quickly over to Kerry's side. A tear traced its way unchecked down Kerry's cheek. She brushed it away angrily with the back of her hand.

'Oh, Rose, I do miss him so! You've no idea. I—I'll die if—if I don't hear something from him soon.'

'I'm sure you'll see him before long. Or you'll get a letter—maybe tomorrow.'

'I've been standing at the window

35

watching for the postman every morning since I wrote to him. It's so awful not to know how he feels about—about it.'

'How do you feel, Kerry?'

Kerry's face was clear and candid. 'You know I never did bother much about babies, Rose—I was never one of those girls who wanted to push other people's offspring out in their prams, didn't even play with dolls much when I was little.'

'I know. We were a couple of tomboys together, always trying to beat the boys at their games—almost made it into the cricket team one summer.'

'Yes.' Kerry's eyes were full of wonder as she looked up at Rose. 'But the strange thing is, I can hardly believe it myself, but I really want this baby! I think loving Jacques has changed me so much—I really, really do want to have it and keep it and love it and see it grow up to look just like Jacques—I know I shouldn't be saying that, because I'm not married and I don't know what Jacques will think. He—he may feel quite differently from me. What do you think, Rose? Do you think he's deliberately not answered my letter since he heard?'

Kerry's eyes pleaded for comfort.

'I can't tell you, Kerry. I've never met

36

Jacques, you know.'

'You'd like him. He's so gentle and he has such a way of making you feel important—I don't know, I often wondered what it would be like to fall in love and now that it's happened, I really can't describe it—but you know what I mean, don't you?'

Rose shook her head. 'I've never felt like that—that I would risk everything for any man. I suppose I never was quite as emotional as you, Kerry.'

'Rubbish. Who was it that climbed that tree to rescue her kitten?'

'That's different. That kitten was my pet, I had to get it down.'

'Because you loved it. I remember how soppy you used to be about animals. What about Charles? Haven't you ever felt you'd do anything for him? Just think, Rose—'

'I don't need to think. Charles is all right, of course. I—I like him, but I haven't seen or heard from him for over a month. He went off on a hitch-hiking holiday across Europe.'

'And haven't you missed him?'

'Well, yes—there wasn't anyone to go out with after he left.'

'Huh!' Kerry tossed her head, scorning

37

such cool feelings. 'Is that all he means to you? There are times when I'm not sure that I *like* Jacques—but I never have any doubt that I *love* him.'

Rose poured herself another cup of tea. 'What did Jacques do—before he was called up, I mean?'

'He worked for the du Caines. It's a sort of family tradition. Did I tell you that his father is manager of their estate here in Chandelle?'

'I should have thought Philippe du Caine would look after things himself.'

'You don't realise what a big enterprise it is. The Château here is only a small part of it. There's a big connection in England where the du Caines control an import and distribution side of the wine trade. They're rich and powerful—that's one of the things that makes Philippe so popular with the ladies. I'll show you—'

Kerry jumped up, searched among a pile of newspapers and magazines lying on a chair and produced an expensive glossy. Quickly she flipped over a few pages.

'Here you are—in the Society column.'

She handed the paper to Rose and there, glowering darkly back at her from the page, resplendent in beautifully cut evening clothes, was Philippe du Caine and hanging on his arm a beautiful blonde.

'She's a French film star, I believe—one of the up and coming—and no doubt it helped her career to have that picture in the papers. He's quite a boy for the ladies, I can tell you.'

Rose felt discomfited by Kerry's repeated assertion. 'I don't know why you keep telling me that, Kerry—I have no interest in him.'

'You can't live in Chandelle and not be interested in the du Caines,' Kerry said airily. 'Mind you, he usually keeps his affairs well away from the Château because he has an elderly maiden aunt there who's a real gorgon by all accounts.'

'I can't imagine Philippe allowing an old aunt to dominate him,' said Rose.

'Ah, but it's not as simple as that,' Kerry said meaningly. 'You see, this old aunt—she really is old, a great-aunt, I believe—yes, she must be, because the story goes that she came to Chandelle after the First World War. Would you believe that! All those years ago—when her sister married Philippe's grandfather. And she's still there, and apparently that marriage made the link between the wine barons here in Chandelle and the big business firm in London, and the great-aunt still controls the purse-strings—you know what I mean?'

'She's a principal shareholder, something like that?'

'Precisely. So you see why Philippe has to behave himself—at least that's how Jacques put it.'

After they had eaten their leisurely meal, they cleared the table and washed up, then made coffee and sat on talking, talking, talking. Kerry brought out a small collection of snapshots, mostly of Jacques. She looked at each one with a loving smile before passing them over to Rose. Jacques had a pleasant face; he was dark-skinned, black-haired, and when he smiled his expression had an engaging merriness.

'I couldn't talk to my parents like this about Jacques,' Kerry said. 'They seemed to quite like him at first, but then when they realised how serious it was between us, they began to change. Then when I had to tell them about the baby they nearly exploded. I know I ought to be sorry, but I can't, I really can't. I wouldn't have done it if I hadn't been so sure of my love. I know there'll never be anyone else for me—if only he'd send word that he feels the same I'd be over the moon, I really would.'

Rose saw the glow on Kerry's face, that could so quickly change to sorrow; the tears were not far from the surface, she was living on a high pitch of emotion. Thank goodness she had answered her friend's call. Kerry really did need her, especially until she heard from Jacques. Meanwhile it seemed to help to talk about him. It was late when they went to bed at last. Rose lay awake for a long time, her mind too active to settle immediately and her emotions stirred by Kerry's words. Would she ever love anyone as Kerry obviously loved Jacques?

She thought of Charles and how he had kissed her that first time, behind the bicycle shed at school—she had thought she was in love then and she had missed him when he set off on his own as soon as the term ended. She had no idea where he was now. Charles was a nice boy, everyone said so. He was the sort of boy her family would be happy for her to marry—but Rose could not help thinking that life with Charles might be just a bit dull. Kerry showed that there could be so much more to love—but perhaps it was not given to every woman to feel such an emotion? She turned over and went to sleep.

In the morning the sun was again beating down from a cloudless sky. Rose and Kerry walked together to the village shops. They were small family businesses set in among the houses, the whole place cheerfully unplanned, doors opened direct to the pavement, steps led to tenements above. There were stalls standing outside the greengrocers, heaped with aubergines, courgettes, melons, apples, bananas, oranges, peppers both red and green, bunches of chives, parsley and other fresh herbs ready for the *bouquet garni* beloved of French cooking, strings of garlic and onions.

The town was so small they could walk the length of it in a mere fifteen minutes. Rose investigated an old public washhouse; relic of the days before automatic washing machines, it utilised a spring of water that came from up in the rock-strewn hills and was channelled through heavy stone bowls. Once the place must have been alive with the chatter of women at their laundry; now it was dank and deserted, the only noise the constant splash of the falling water. In some ways the village seemed to have close links with the Middle Ages, in others it was very much in the twentieth century. Rose bought some postcards. She avoided those with pictures of the Château, though she would have found it difficult to explain her reason for this. Certainly those photographs were among the most attractive of the display, though there were some delightful scenes which included the church with its painted statue outside. There had been no letter for Kerry; they had both seen the yellow post office van pass by without stopping. Rose felt deeply sorry as Kerry tried to hide her disappointment.

'Shall we go to the river to swim and sunbathe this afternoon?' Kerry suggested.

'Sounds great.'

They changed into bikinis in their bedrooms. Rose had a white two-piece, she had never worn it before and it was more scanty than her previous one had been. She hesitated even now as she stepped into it and fastened the bra behind her. Anxiously she turned in front of the mirror—was it too daring? She called Kerry to give her opinion. Kerry came in wearing a bikini that was of about identical size but of flame colour material.

'You look great, Rose—' Kerry began.

'That's just what I'm afraid of,' Rose replied. 'How great? Like an elephant?'

Kerry laughed. 'Rose! You always did twist anything I said. Everyone wears them like that now, in fact a lot of the girls don't wear tops at all.'

'I've heard of topless sunbathing, but I wasn't sure how openly it was done.'

'Perfectly all right, I assure you,' Kerry said airily. 'I've often sunbathed topless myself, especially when Jacques was here— he liked me to be brown all over—well, almost all over. Oh, don't look so shocked, Rose. I won't do it today, I don't like to when we haven't got a man with us, other men can sometimes take the wrong meaning.'

'I could imagine that,' said Rose drily.

'You should try it some day,' Kerry insisted. 'It's a great feeling, having the sun to kiss your whole body—and when you swim it's so free. I don't know—I think the French are far less inhibited about nudity than we British are.'

'I—I don't know—' Rose hesitated.

'Anyway, I doubt if there'll be anyone else about down at the river this afternoon.

It's always quiet, the tourists haven't really discovered this part of the country and the locals are either away on holiday or working. There may be a few children, otherwise we'll have the place to ourselves, I expect. Come on!'

They both put light cotton dresses over their bikinis and taking towels to lie on, books, tanning oils, sunglasses, shady hats and a couple of cans of lemonade, set out for the river. An elderly lady in a black and white dress and a straw hat shaped like a topee was gathering haricot beans in the next garden. She called out a friendly greeting to Kerry, who briefly introduced her to Rose and told her they were going for a swim.

The path took them up the hill behind the house, then dropped down a grassy slope to a valley where the river flowed and eddied along a wide tree-bordered bed. Rough steps led from the bank to a beach of smooth-worn rocks and yellowish stones. Rocks and gravel shone through the translucent freshness of the water. Upstream there was a weir which held back the flow, the sluice gates allowing only a gentle overspill down its weed-washed wall. It looked cool and inviting on that brilliant hot day, and at once they stripped off their dresses and waded in.

'It shelves sharply over there, but we can swim across to those rocks by the weir,' Kerry pointed out.

The current was quite powerful in one place, but they were both good swimmers and soon they were into shallow water again, wading out to stand on the high flat rocks from which the weir stretched across the river. It was a delightful place, so secluded, and as Kerry had anticipated there was no one else there that day. They swam back to the beach and stretched out on their towels to dry off and soak up some sun. Kerry soon dropped off to sleep, and Rose opened her book.

It was perhaps half an hour later that she heard a footstep on the stones close by, and she looked up and saw a young man in military uniform walking towards them. She recognised him at once from the photographs Kerry had shown her last night and was about to waken her friend, but Jacques put a finger to his lips, smiling mischievously. He knelt beside Kerry and lightly brushed her cheek with his lips, and as he did so he murmured her name softly.

'Kérie!'

He pronounced it as if it rhymed with *chérie,* and that touch of accent made the name itself into an endearment. Kerry stirred, looked up sleepily, then opened her eyes wide with joy and disbelief, flinging her arms up to encircle the khaki-clad figure. They kissed and Rose turned away, sitting up now, clasping her knees, looking steadfastly towards the river.

'Rose—this is Jacques,' said Kerry, unnecessarily, a moment later.

They shook hands. Jacques knew very little English and Kerry's French was rather halting, but language was obviously no barrier to their love. Jacques had managed to wangle a couple of days' leave and had driven down to Chandelle as fast as possible after receiving Kerry's letter. He had not even stopped to eat on the journey, so they went up to the villa to find some food.

Hand in hand the young lovers walked away from the beach. Rose elected to stay on by the river, knowing they wanted to be alone. She felt an immense relief, all would now be well with Kerry. Jacques had not let her down, his love for her was as strong as hers for him—that had been apparent in those brief moments of greeting. Left to herself, Rose decided to take another swim. She amused herself in the shallows for a quarter of an hour or so, then swam across to those flat rocks beside the weir.

It was blissfully lonely there; apart from Jacques no one had come near the river for the past hour. Rose stretched out on the rocks and, emboldened by the isolation of the place, decided to remove her bikini top. She stretched out and gloried in the sun's embracing warmth on her body, bare but for her small briefs. The rocks were warm to her back, the sun dancing on her legs, her flat stomach, her breasts and her face. A deliciously sensual feeling crept over her, as if she was a lizard, almost as naturally naked as a wild creature. She closed her eyes feeling completely relaxed, she smiled as she recalled the rapture in Kerry's face as she was awakened by Jacques' kiss and she drifted off to sleep.

It was a shadow falling over her face that wakened her, and she opened her eyes and gasped. There standing on the rocks looking down at her was—Philippe du Caine! He moved slightly and as the shadow passed from her face the sun shone blindingly into her eyes, making him a huge dark towering form above her. She noticed the glint of droplets of water that trickled down his bare, tanned shoulders, but the expression of his face was shaded from her.

She didn't wait to look more closely. Horrified at her topless state, she reached out quickly to where she had left her bikini bra and in a single movement had it hugged across her bare breasts. He sat down on a slightly higher rock close by and she saw that he was smiling, amused at her embarrassment.

'I didn't intend to startle you, Rose,' he said.

She was struggling to fasten the hook at the back. Although her breasts were now covered she felt as naked as ever, knowing he had stood there looking at her—for how long? She might have been sleeping still if his shadow had not fallen over her face—how dared he take advantage of her like that? Angrily she scrambled to her feet. She had only one thought, to get away from him. He had unnerved her, what did he want?

'You have no need to be embarrassed—'

'I thought I was alone here.'

'That was obvious. You are not accustomed to topless sunbathing, are you, Rose? But it is done everywhere nowadays.'

His words told her he had indeed been regarding her closely; he had noticed the pale skin of her breasts in comparison with the rest of her body. But, as he pointed out, it was by no means unusual for girls to go topless these days, it was only that she was unused to it. He obviously was well used to seeing girls in such a state, no doubt he had been assessing her assets as against those of others.

'You have a lovely body, Rose. It was indeed a delight to come up out of the river and find such a mermaid lying on the rocks.'

Rose was struggling to regain her equilibrium. She looked at him. Droplets of water still clung to his tanned skin, matted the hair on his powerful chest, trickled down the flatness of his muscled stomach and pencilled fine lines on his long, strong legs. Now she could see his face, his expression was calm, relaxed in contrast to her own disturbed emotions, his eyes dark, unfathomable, his mouth set in a straight well-controlled line.

'Were—were you swimming here, just by

chance?' she asked.

'No, I came to find you.'

'Oh.' She waited for him to explain.

'Your friend said you were sunbathing and your things were on the beach. Actually I was not at that time sure whether you had gone for a walk or what, so as I had my trunks in the car close by, I decided to have a swim myself. This stretch of river has always been one of my favourite places since I was a boy.'

He spoke quite matter-of-factly now, as if he wanted to soothe her, and Rose began to feel calmer, though she was still on the defensive.

'Why did you wish to see me?' she asked.

'Simply to tell you that your car is almost ready. I telephoned the garage, they have managed to get the spare parts and it can be collected tomorrow afternoon.'

'That's wonderful!'

'I shall be going into Les Virages then, so I will take you over and you can drive it back.'

She was touched by his thoughtfulness. 'That's very kind of you—if you're sure it won't be any trouble—'

He held up a hand to cut short her protests.

'We won't go into that again. You know there are no buses. I'll be leaving at about two-thirty, I'll pick you up at the villa, or you can walk up to the Château if you like.'

Anxious to cause him the minimum of inconvenience, she said, 'I'll walk up to the Château. Thank you very much.'

No doubt he was going into Les Virages to visit, as Kerry had put it, 'one of his mistresses'. Rose imagined that the girl he loved there would be sophisticated, not at all ordinary and naïve as she was, but she appreciated the kindness that had prompted him to make the enquiry about her car and arrange to take her to pick it up. She ought to have been more gracious to him—but he was such a disturbing man. Every time they met she seemed to have placed herself at a disadvantage through her own foolishness. He stood up.

'I think it's time we went back,' he said.

'There's no hurry for me,' she replied.

In answer he reached out a hand and gently touched her shoulder. Her skin burned, and she recoiled from him.

'You see? You are not accustomed to our French sunshine—you will get sore if you stay out here much longer.'

It had not been simply the sun that had caused that tingling of her flesh, but she couldn't tell him that. His touch had been the merest brush of his fingers.

'Come,' he said, pulling her to her feet. 'We'll swim back together.'

He dived off the rocks and Rose followed him into the water, surfacing closer to him than she had expected. He was treading water, waiting for her, and together they swam into the deeper part, farther upstream than she had been before, and there it seemed the current swirled rather more strongly. The force of the water caught her off guard and she felt her arm and then her leg brush against Philippe's. It was like an electric shock sweeping over her, making her miss her stroke—she wanted desperately to escape from that nearness, but he seemed to enjoy the touch and stayed close to her.

The force of the water exhilarated her, again she had that feeling of being a wild creature—a mermaid, he had called her. She laughed out loud, making a game of it, and dived below the surface, thinking to escape but still he swam beside her, as close as ever, and as she surfaced she felt her body brush against his yet again.

'Sorry—' she began to apologise, but the words were drowned.

Philippe's arms closed about her and stroked liquidly down the length of her from shoulder to thigh. She struggled, but her efforts seemed only to bring her closer into the circle of his hold, and then he kissed her. His mouth was sweet and damp with the river water, his lips pressing hard against hers with a practised sensuality that left her breathless.

Suddenly she knew that he thought she had been deliberately provocative and she twisted from the clasp of his arms and swam with all her strength for the beach. He followed immediately and, since he was a stronger swimmer than she was, soon caught up with her.

'Stay in the water, Rose—'

'No!'

She thought he would reach out for her again. She swam on, her arms flailing with almost a panic, but though he stayed alongside her until they were out of the deep water he remained an arm's length away, making no further attempt to touch her.

As soon as the water was shallow enough Rose stood up and ran out and wrapped her towel close around her, needing its comfort even though the day was still warm, simply to hide herself from him. She was shaking so much that her knees felt weak and she sat down abruptly, still closely covered by the towel. The grit in it scratched her reddening shoulders. Philippe pulled on a tee-shirt and a pair of shorts over his wet swimming trunks. His casualness made her more angry.

'You had no right to—to do that!' the words burst out fast and furious. 'I must let you know that I—I'm just not that sort of girl!'

He regarded her with a faint smile twisting one corner of his lips, then he bowed mockingly.

'My apologies, Rose Robinson.' He had a way of saying her name that made it sound so beautiful she could scarcely believe it belonged to her. 'I do not usually misread gestures from women.'

He paused, watching her closely, and Rose felt the colour rush into her cheeks. If she was honest with herself she had to admit that his kiss, lightly playful as it had been, had thrilled her in a way that had never happened before. It had been her own response that had frightened her. She looked at him with a gaze she intended to be haughty, dismissing him as a mere man. The twinkle in his eyes was disconcerting.

'Shall we say we were both caught off guard out there?'

Without waiting for her to reply he strode away, up the beach, mounted the steps two at a time. He paused at the top and turned briefly back to her.

'See you tomorrow afternoon—about two-thirty.'

Then he disappeared into a belt of trees.

CHAPTER THREE

Rose walked up the road to the Château in good time the following afternoon, determined not to keep Philippe waiting. She had deliberately pushed those disturbing incidents with him to the back of her mind. No doubt this afternoon he would be preoccupied with his visit to the lady in Les Virages, whoever she was. For her own part Rose had made up her mind to keep remote from him, giving him no opportunity for a repeat of any flirtation.

Last evening at the villa with Kerry and Jacques had been fun—they were so happy to be together, so content that the linking of their lives would now have to be made official. It was late when Jacques left and he had turned up at the villa again in the middle of the morning. Kerry blossomed now that her lover was beside her again; she was so much like her old self that Rose could not help catching something of her gaiety. They all ate lunch together, picnic style, in the garden. Now Jacques and Kerry were tackling the washing up, shooing Rose away when she offered to help, making the dull chore into a magical piece of togetherness, like two children playing at houses.

The road to the Château wound up away from the village and entered the grounds via tall wrought iron gates which were permanently open, set in a high stone wall. The gardens were terraced in front of the big old house which suddenly came in sight, a mass of ochre and cream stone, rising with rounded towers on either side, rows of beautifully proportioned windows were set in its façade and a wide flight of steps, flanked by lions couchant, led to wide double doors. It seemed to be a mixture of styles; there was something Georgian in the main part of the building, but the towers were medieval in appearance with narrow slits, defensive-looking, rising high above the main roof and topped with conical roofs, grey-slated, finished by ornamental bosses.

Rose approached slowly, looking with admiration at the formal gardens laid out in front of the Château, beds bright with salvias, marigolds and gladioli edged by close-clipped box borders. There was an ornamental pool in the centre, with a Grecian style statue of a goddess holding a water jug from which poured a cascade of water. It fell with a cool, tinkling splash back into the pool below and Rose caught a glimpse of darting goldfish. Beyond the formal terrace to the side of the Château she noticed a swimming pool surrounded by lush green lawns which must have been constantly watered to retain such verdure in the hot, dry climate.

As she neared the front steps, hesitating whether to mount them and ring the bell to make her presence known, Rose saw the door open and an elderly lady came out. She was accompanied by a golden retriever which she held on a harness. The dog looked at Rose and gave a gruff bark, then it walked slowly forward towards the side of the steps. The lady paused there and stretched out her hand towards the balustrade.

'Good afternoon,' said Rose, stepping forward.

'Good afternoon. Are you waiting for Philippe?'

Holding the balustrade with one hand and the dog's harness in the other, she made her way with precision down the steps to where Rose stood at the bottom. As she watched the careful descent of the steps Rose suddenly realised that the lady was blind, yet she was negotiating her way so confidently with the aid of the dog and the balustrade that at first glance it had not struck her what the abnormality was. Now that the lady was closer she could see that the eyes had a glazed, blue appearance and that they were fixed on the distance beyond her.

When Rose answered they came into focus again and it would have been difficult to be sure whether she could see or not.

'Yes. Monsieur du Caine is taking me into Les Virages to pick up my car.'

'Ah, you are the young English lady?'

Until then they had been speaking in French. Now the lady changed into English, speaking it clearly but with just that same trace of accent that Philippe had.

'Yes. I'm staying with a friend in the village.'

'Philippe told me. Now what did he say your name was? You must forgive me, I should have remembered—'

She held out her hand as she spoke. Rose took it and felt the delicacy of the old bones in her grasp, but the fingers closed on hers with surprising strength. There was power in this frail old lady.

'Rose Robinson,' she introduced herself.

'I'm Celia Grantchester. I'm Philippe's great-aunt. Do you know I've lived here in this old house since 1920? So long—such a long, long time.'

'You must have been back to England sometimes since then?' Rose asked.

60

'But of course, Rose—do you mind if I call you Rose?'

Evidently she assumed that consent was given, as indeed it was, though she could not have seen Rose nod her head. Without pausing she went on.

'Naturally I've been back to England many times, but I don't go so often now; it's too much effort to make the journey. Besides, I feel more at home here. I get lost when I'm away from the Château. I'm blind, you know. Not completely, of course, I can tell when the sun's shining brightly like it is today and I can see you standing there, though only vaguely. I'll have to ask Philippe what you look like. Let's go and sit on the seat over there. If you'll take my arm, Rose, I'll let Gigi off her harness.'

Miss Grantchester needed little guiding, she knew exactly where the seat was, and as she sat down and patted the place beside her for Rose to sit she said,

'Yes, it was in 1920 when I came to the Château. You see, my sister married Philippe's grandfather in that year. She was very beautiful and rather delicate, and she found it very difficult to fit into this hot climate and the ways of the French and she was so homesick she sent for me. I came just for a holiday, but there were so many things I could do to help that I just stayed on and on. It was just as well I did as events turned out. You see, my dear Lucy was so very delicate. We all thought she would die when Philippe's father was born and Lucy just could not cope with the antics of a small boy, and so I stayed.'

'That must have been a great help to everyone,' Rose murmured.

'I hope so. I think it must have been, otherwise I should have gone back to England. You look back at your life and wonder where it has all gone. But I know I have been useful—and I've had a happy life too, in spite of everything. I brought Philippe up too, you know.'

'Did you?'

Miss Grantchester needed little encouragement to talk.

'It was terrible—terrible! His parents were both killed in an air crash. Of course that was a long time ago now, Philippe was so young he can scarcely remember them. I'd been thinking that perhaps I should return to London, but I hadn't done anything about it. Château

Chandelle is a pleasant place to live, but I've been very lucky, you know. What was I telling you, Rose?'

'How you looked after Philippe.'

'That's right. He went to one of the best public schools in England—I saw to that. His grandfather wanted him to be educated in France, but I pointed out to him that if Philippe was to take over the business in both countries he must speak perfect English. He was a wonderful boy—'

'Is that you telling tales out of school, Aunt Celia?'

Philippe's voice interrupted her. He stood on the steps above them; neither had heard him approach.

'I've just been entertaining Rose. You shouldn't keep a young lady waiting, you know, Philippe.'

'It's my fault—I was early,' said Rose.

Aunt Celia took hold of her hand. 'I'm glad you were early. I've enjoyed talking to you. You must dine with us tonight—mustn't she, Philippe?'

Philippe said, 'I'm afraid I shan't be back for dinner tonight, Aunt Celia.'

Aunt Celia tossed her head as if that answer angered her. 'Does that mean you're staying in Les Virages?' There was no mistaking the criticism in her voice. 'You shouldn't do it, Philippe. Think of your position.'

'This is one point on which I cannot expect you to agree with me,' Philippe answered. He walked across to stand beside Miss Grantchester. 'I'm glad Rose will be dining with you, Aunt. Another time in the future I shall be here to share that pleasure with you, but for this evening I must decline. I have a prior engagement.'

'Well, if I can't persuade you to see reason—'

'On this point we must differ, Aunt Celia.'

He leaned over and kissed his great-aunt on the cheek. Affectionate though he was towards his aunt, he evidently had no intention of giving up this affair he was carrying on in Les Virages to please her.

'Young men are all the same,' grumbled Miss Grantchester. 'Always so headstrong, always letting their emotions rule their heads.'

Philippe had not stopped to hear her; doubtless it was an old argument. He was walking towards his car, parked in the drive. Rose stood up.

'I must go now.'

'Dinner's at eight. I'll expect you half an hour before then for an *apéritif.*'

Rose felt she had had little chance to refuse, but since Philippe would not be there she was quite happy to accede to the acceptance that had been automatically attributed to her. She ran towards the car, where Philippe waited, holding open the passenger door. Soon they were driving towards Les Virages.

'What a charming lady your great-aunt is,' Rose remarked.

'I'm glad you like her. She's a pretty marvellous person—I owe her a lot.'

But you won't give up this liaison of which she disapproves, thought Rose. There was silence between them for a short time, then he asked,

'Did she tell you how she came to the Château in 1920?'

'I gathered it was as a companion to her sister when she married your grandfather.'

'That's right. I always think that was more like a business merger than a marriage. It linked the two firms together, the wine-growers on the French side and the importing and distributing firm in London. It was however, highly successful, both from a financial and from a matri-monial point of view.'

'You make it sound like a cold-blooded calculation,' Rose protested.

'It was. Both my grandmother and Aunt Celia had been engaged to young men who were killed in the First World War. I believe the suggested marriage to my grandfather came as something of a bonus to them both, they led a very cloistered existence in London with a tyrannical Victorian father. Château Chandelle was an escape, and my grandfather was quite an amiable sort of man. The marriage worked, I am sure of that.'

'You don't think that love came into it?'

'Initially almost certainly it did not—but yes, I believe there must have been a—a liking, a respect, and out of that it is possible that over the years some affection grew. They were both still alive when I was a child—I assure you there was an atmosphere of happy calm between them. It was evident in the whole household, that's why I say it was such a successful marriage. Do you not think that is something of an achievement?'

'Possibly. But I would never marry without love.'

'Ah, but what is love?'

Rather than admit that she had never really been in love Rose answered, 'It's a deep, fulfilling emotion that binds you to someone so that to you they seem special.'

'Is that all?'

'Isn't it enough? It makes young men write poetry and makes young women beautiful, it makes the whole world blossom.'

A smile twisted a corner of his mouth.

'Then I will write a poem to you, Rose—what would you say if I did that?'

She laughed, knowing he was teasing her. 'It would depend on what you wrote, and whether you really meant it.'

'But how would you know? You see, take the case of my grandfather again. I suppose he could have written poems to my grandmother or paid someone else to write them and pretended they were from him—'

'That would have been dishonest.'

'Precisely. But because he made an honest offer of marriage, just that and no more, the deal was satisfactory to both parties. And incidentally, my aunt benefited too, because her life here was much freer and more full and satisfying than it would have been had she remained in that stuffy London house. We use it as an office nowadays, and I have a flat on the top floor, but I am always glad to escape back to Chandelle.'

'The Château is so lovely, I suppose that would help to make up for the lack of love,' Rose suggested.

'Then you admit that a *marriage de convenance* could be satisfactory, given the right conditions?'

'Possibly it could for some people—but not for me. When I marry it will be for love alone.'

'Like Kerry and Jacques? Do you think that this great love of theirs which is rushing them into marriage is such a good basis for happiness? For my part I would prefer a calmly arranged contract.'

Rose glanced sharply across at him. She had not realised that he knew about Kerry and Jacques. Then she remembered that Jacques' father was Philippe's manager and guessed that he had been told—probably only this morning, for surely Jacques' parents had not even known until yesterday evening.

'I know they are happy now,' she said.

'So you approve of what they have done?'

'I didn't say that.'

'And yet you rush down to back them up.'

'Kerry is my friend, of course I came when she needed me.'

There was a hard set line to Philippe's face, but what right had he to be displeased? Was he not himself engaged in an illicit affair? The love of Kerry and Jacques might be precipitate, but it was open and caring. She tossed her head with a touch of defiance.

'I think they'll be all right. I know they're very much in love.'

'Love can be bitter as well as sweet, do you not think so, Rose?'

'I—I don't know.'

He glanced at her and his expression was enigmatic.

'One day I am sure you will know. Perhaps I shall ask you that question again—some other time.'

Pertly she chipped back at him, 'And when I learn that you are to be married I will know that it's simply a business arrangement, just another contract to be signed.'

'One thing I do believe is that such a contract is binding and that it is for life.'

'You're thinking of getting married, then?'

'It is a thought that has occurred to me,' he replied, so noncommittally that his answer was meaningless.

He drove on to the forecourt of the garage and stopped the car. He turned and looked fully at her. She was sitting well away from him, had almost hugged the passenger door for the whole of the journey, taking elaborate care never to allow herself to slide towards him, mindful of how their bodies had brushed together when they were swimming and of the magnetism that had seemed to make contact almost inevitable. She could not deny the strong attraction of this virile man who was looking at her with those mocking brown eyes, as if he challenged her—challenged her to what? Was it simply that he was so conscious of his power over women that he had to prove himself with each and every one? Whatever it was she was determined to fight it. She turned away from him and fumbled with the fastening of the door.

'Thank you for the lift,' she said with a coolness she was far from feeling.

He got out and came round to open the door for her, then escorted her across to the garage where he had a conversation with the mechanic. Rose listened and gathered that all was satisfactory. She paid the bill with traveller's cheques, and only after Philippe had walked with her to the little green Mini did he allow himself to be dismissed. His manners, she had to admit, were impeccable, and his courtesy and kindness really more than she deserved. There was something even a little old-fashioned in his concern to ensure that the car was quite in order; probably that was due to being brought up by grandparents and an elderly aunt, as well as to that formidable public school. But charming though it was, Rose sensed again that hint of patronage in his attitude, that strong masculine ego that still made him regard her as nothing but a silly girl-child.

As she drove back along the road to Chandelle Rose thought over their conversation and wished she had been able to make bright and clever replies, the sort of thing that his sophisticated lady friends would undoubtedly have said. How she regretted her youth and her lack of experience! If only she could some time meet Philippe du Caine on his own level, if only he did not always leave her feeling that she was still just a rather foolish schoolgirl. She felt, however, that she had learned a bit more about him—and decided that attractive though he undoubtedly was, he was not a really pleasant young man. She was glad to have the Mini back; her grandmother had said, 'It will give you independence,' and that was true. One thing was certain—she would not have to rely on Philippe for transport again.

There was no need to hurry back to Chandelle. Kerry and Jacques would be more than happy to be alone together and she was not due to visit Miss Grantchester till about seven-thirty. She had noticed a route marked as of scenic interest which was a roundabout way of returning, and she took this. The road rose on an incline winding through wooded countryside, then it dropped to the valley of the river. Rose stopped the car and got out at a vantage point.

She sat on a low stone wall and gazed down at the river. Wide and shallow, it meandered through meadows where white Charollais cattle grazed. Beyond, terraced up a hillside, were rows and rows of vines. The humming of the *cigales* rose in a crescendo that almost drowned the gurgling of the river, otherwise there was peace—no sound of traffic, no voice of human. Rose sat on in the sunshine for so long that a lizard ventured out of a crack in the rocks to bask in the sun beside her. It reminded her of her own sunbathing yesterday when she had lain so nearly naked on those rocks—even the memory was embarrassing. She moved, and the lizard darted away, as startled as she had been when Philippe had found her there.

She walked back to the car and drove on. She stopped at a village where there was an *auberge* and ordered a *citron pressé*, a delicious drink made from fresh lemons, sugar and soda. She sat outside the café, but remembering she had been slightly sunburned yesterday and that the sun was still very hot, chose a shady spot. Inside the café a group of elderly men were whiling away the afternoon with a game of cards and a few drinks. The landlady stood and chatted with her in friendly fashion—strangers were made welcome in those parts. It was almost seven when Rose returned to the villa. Kerry called out as she walked into the house.

'Rose? Thank goodness—I was afraid we'd be late.'

'Late for what?'

'We're going to visit Jacques' parents.'

'That's okay. You won't need me, and I've been invited to dine with Miss Grantchester.'

'Oh no!' Kerry's face fell. 'I was counting on you coming with us, Rose. Your French is so much better than mine, and you must have noticed Jacques' English is almost non-existent.'

'I'm sure you'll manage, Kerry.'

'I feel so awful about everything. I mean, I do so want them to like me—'

'I'm sure they will,' Rose reassured her. 'Just be your usual nice cheery self.'

'But I don't *feel* my usual bright cheery self, as you put it. I feel terrible. I'm petrified at the thought of going up there.'

'Haven't you met them before?'

'Only very briefly. And then Jacques and I were just friends—now everything's different. Can't you dine with Miss Grantchester another time?'

Rose shook her head. 'I don't think I could do that. It was kind of her to invite

74

me, and besides, if I don't go she'll be left on her own.'

Kerry still pouted with disappointment and Rose could tell that she was really troubled about the evening ahead. She suggested the only solution she could think of.

'Perhaps I can come to Jacques' house later on—after dinner. I dare say Miss Grantchester won't stay up very late. She'll probably be glad if I leave at about nine-thirty.'

Kerry seized on the suggestion eagerly.

'Oh yes, please, Rose. It'll help me no end if I know you'll be there eventually.'

'I doubt if you'll need me—by that time you'll have completely charmed them.'

'I have the feeling they think I'm a proper little scrubber,' said Kerry ruefully.

'Nonsense! Get that idea out of your head immediately, Kerry. You've been foolish, that I will agree, but you and Jacques love each other, that's what counts.'

Kerry tried a watery smile.

'That's better.' Rose gave her a quick hug. 'Now I must get tidied up.'

She had a bath and changed into a becoming dress in a flowing voile material, patterned with pink roses and a tracery of dark grey foliage, she clasped a shiny black belt around her narrow waist, added a pretty chain bracelet and a tiny gold crucifix pendant. She brushed her hair till it shone and the waves deepened; the touch of sunburn had muted to a becoming light tan which added lustre to her healthy face. It was characteristic of her to dress with care, though Miss Grantchester would not be able to see her, and she would have done the same even if she had not promised to call in on Jacques' parents. She carried a white crocheted stole in case the air should turn chilly and a tiny silver evening bag.

A maid opened the door of the Château in answer to the bell and ushered Rose into a huge dark-panelled hallway. A wide staircase rose towards the far wall, where halfway up an arched recess held a lifesize Grecian statue; there the stairs divided into two flights to sweep away at right angles on up to a gallery that overlooked the hall on two sides. Rose gave the maid a friendly smile as she walked through a side door that was held open for her.

'Mademoiselle Robinson,' the maid announced.

Miss Grantchester was seated on a comfortable chintz-covered settee, her dog lying at her feet, her hands holding a Braille book. She set this aside and Rose moved over to her and shook the hand that was outstretched. The dog opened one enquiring eye and thumped her tail a couple of times as if registering approval.

'Come and sit beside me, Rose. What will you have to drink?'

'Nothing, thank you, Miss Grantchester.'

'Not even a small sherry?'

'I—I don't really like it.'

'Then of course you're quite right not to take it—but you will allow me to have one. Yvette—' she addressed the maid who was already setting a small table close to Miss Grantchester, 'I'll have my usual.'

'*Oui, mademoiselle.*'

Yvette poured the golden liquid into a delicately cut glass and directed her mistress's hand to show her exactly where it was placed on a coaster. Miss Grantchester raised the glass and took an appreciative sip.

'I don't drink a great deal, but I do enjoy a sherry before my evening meal,' she remarked. 'Now let me see—you were going with Philippe to fetch your car. Did you have a pleasant trip?'

Rose remembered the conversation she had had and the differences of opinion that always seemed to arise when she was with Philippe du Caine, but she had no intention of going over that with his great-aunt.

'Yes indeed—and it was so kind of Monsieur du Caine to take me to the garage to fetch my car.'

'He's very thoughtful. I notice it particularly since I lost my sight. Nothing is too much trouble for him—I often think how lucky I am to have such a nephew. If he were my own grandson he couldn't be more kind to me.'

'I'm sure he's very fond of you, Miss Grantchester,' Rose agreed.

'Did he tell you why he was going to Les Virages?'

Rose was startled. 'No, I—I have no idea.'

She stumbled over the words, surprised at the question. She had assumed from what Kerry had said that Miss Grantchester would not wish such a subject to be broached.

'No, I don't suppose he would.' The lady's voice had a prim, disapproving note.

'I'm almost a stranger to him really.' Rose felt she must explain. Somehow Miss Grantchester seemed to have read something much deeper into the simple offer of a lift. 'We only met by chance when my car broke down. I'm staying with a friend in the village.'

'Yes, of course.' Miss Grantchester's face relaxed. 'Tell me something about yourself. I know you're pretty because Philippe told me, and I know you're very young—'

'I'm almost nineteen,' said Rose, and was glad that Miss Grantchester could not see that she was blushing, surprised that Philippe had been talking to his aunt about her.

'Where do you live in England?'

Rose told her, and as the old lady was so interested she expanded and talked about her parents and her grandmother and Kerry and Jacques, though she omitted to mention the reason why the wedding was to be rather hurried.

On the dot of eight o'clock the maid came in and announced that dinner was served. She removed the little table and placed it carefully beside the wall, and Miss Grantchester rose to her feet and negotiated the furniture to reach the door so skilfully that it was difficult to remember that she could not see. Rose followed her into the dining-room; it was large and grand, but their meal had been set at only one end of the long polished table. The furniture was antique Louis Quinze, and three tall windows opened to the lawns beyond and the swimming pool Rose had noticed earlier.

Miss Grantchester took her place at the head of the table and Rose sat on her right. A delicious pâté was already served for the first course, the plate garnished with lettuce and tomato—there were flowers on the table and a huge bowl of fruit, the silver gleamed and the napery was crisply laundered. Whether Miss Grantchester could see or not, there was no lowering of standards.

'I hope you will like the pâté, it's a speciality of the region,' Miss Grantchester told her.

'Delicious,' Rose assured her, taking a little on her fork.

'Food is one of my great pleasures, my dear. Not too much of it, you understand, but small quantities of really excellent cuisine—that is one of my greatest joys nowadays, and we are fortunate to have a wonderful chef. He's been with the family for several years now and knows just how I like things.'

The meal was exquisite in every mouth-watering detail, each course lingered over and savoured and the conversation between them flowed easily and amusingly so that Rose felt as if she had known Miss Grantchester for a long time instead of meeting her for the first time that day. The rapport was completely reciprocated, for as they returned to the lounge for coffee Miss Grantchester remarked, 'My dear, I can't remember when I've taken to anyone so quickly before. I do hope I haven't bored you?'

'I've enjoyed every minute,' Rose replied truthfully.

She glanced at her watch and saw that it was already ten past nine. She remembered her promise to call in on Jacques' parents, but it would not be polite to leave yet; besides, Miss Grantchester was wide awake showing no sign of flagging as she chatted on and on and it would be unthinkable to leave her too abruptly after she had been so kind.

'I wish you would come and see me more often, Rose. I hesitate to ask, because

81

I know how busy you young people are these days, but would it be possible for you to help me with some correspondence and read to me in English? My secretary has had to leave because her husband's job has taken them to Paris, and it's not easy to get someone to replace her here in Chandelle. Besides, I would so like to hear some of my favourite poems read in English, and you have a lovely voice.'

'Why, I'd be delighted to do that.'

So they fell to discussing poetry, and though there was such a great age difference they found that their tastes for the romantic were similar. Yvette brought in a tray of coffee, poured out two cups and plugged in the percolator to keep it warm. Rose noticed that another cup was set on the tray and a short time later, as if he was expected, Philippe walked in. He had changed from the casual clothes he had worn that afternoon into a lightweight beige-coloured suit, a cream shirt and a tie that incorporated both those shades with a deeper brown. Miss Grantchester knew he was there immediately he opened the door—and Rose felt she would also have sensed his presence, even if she had not seen him; he seemed to dominate the room from the moment he entered.

'Philippe? You're home early,' said Miss Grantchester. 'Just in time to join us for coffee.'

'What a good idea. And have you two had a pleasant evening?'

He moved across to the tray on the side table and helped himself.

'I've enjoyed myself enormously,' said Miss Grantchester. 'And I've persuaded Rose to come up and read to me sometimes.'

'Excellent!'

There was an expression of warm approval on Philippe's face as he turned towards Rose. They talked for a short time longer, then Rose mentioned that she had promised to call in on Jacques' parents.

'Kerry was nervous at meeting them and she particularly asked me to call in. She seemed to think I might be able to interpret, but I'm sure that won't be necessary really.'

Rose stood up and shook hands with her hostess, thanking her sincerely for a very pleasant evening. Philippe also rose to his feet.

'I quite understand. I shall retire soon in any case,' said Miss Grantchester. 'Philippe will accompany you.'

'There's no need,' Rose said quickly. 'I know the way—Kerry explained which is the house.'

'But of course Philippe will go with you,' said Miss Grantchester. 'It will be dark by now—'

'I don't mind in the least,' Rose protested.

Philippe shot her a glance that was a mixture of amusement and displeasure.

'Rose likes to be independent,' he murmured.

'Nonsense,' reiterated Miss Grantchester. 'It wouldn't be seemly for a young lady to be walking about on her own after dark. Now off you go, and no more silly arguing.'

Rose was not at all sure that she welcomed this prospect of a walk through the dark village in the company of this man she found so very disturbing, but he held open the door for her and she knew it would be useless to protest further. In the hall he took the woollen stole she was carrying and gently placed it around her shoulders, and she felt the warmth of his hands and their firm pressure as momentarily he allowed them to linger.

Then, as one accustomed to performing such gallantries, he lifted her hair and arranged it to fall outside the stole. The touch was a reminder that he had been escort to some of the most beautiful women in France. The photograph in the society magazine had portrayed a lady in a mink jacket—no doubt he had placed it there with the same gallant precision and possibly bent his head as he did so to kiss the soft skin of her neck—Rose pulled herself sharply together.

'Thanks,' she said briefly.

He opened the outer door and she stepped out into the darkness of the mild summer night. The air was still and soft, their feet crunched on the gravel, side by side they walked towards the drive and she scarcely knew whether to be glad or sorry that Philippe kept his distance.

'My aunt seems to have taken quite a fancy to you, Rose,' he remarked.

'She's quite charming—it's so sad that she's lost her sight. Can nothing be done about it?'

'There is an operation that might give her back partial sight, but it is only a fifty-fifty chance of success and so far she has not opted to risk it. She can still see a little, in bright sunlight she can even make out the vague form of someone standing beside her. She knows if the day is bright or dull, and she says that life is so full and happy, she should not tempt fate by trying to take more.'

'That's quite a philosophy,' commented Rose.

'She really feels that—that she has so much to be thankful for. She reads Braille, she listens to the radio, she has a garden planted with aromatic herbs and flowers, she does basketwork—and most important of all she keeps in close contact with the business and keeps us all on our toes.'

Rose remembered that Kerry had said that Miss Grantchester held a controlling interest in the family business—from the way Philippe talked he did not seem to resent this as had been implied, but even if he did he would be unlikely to reveal such feelings to a stranger.

The house of Jacques' parents was situated close to where the drive from the Château joined the road to the village. Rose expected that Philippe would bid her goodnight after they had knocked on the door, but to her surprise, when it was opened by Jacques, Philippe followed her inside. They went up a flight of stairs to a large living-room on the first floor, a gracious room furnished in modern style, though from outside the house had looked quite unprepossessing.

Kerry, sitting rather upright, looked close to tears and Jacques' mother, a perky little woman, was red-eyed as if she actually had been crying. His father, a short thick-set man with a double chin and rounded stomach, wore a troubled and angry expression. Rose had the distinct impression that all was far from well, that they had in fact interrupted an angry and emotional scene. Jacques introduced her, and as she shook hands with Monsieur and Madame Vieilland, Philippe appeared in the doorway and was greeted with some surprise, a great deal of pleasure and a certain deference. If he sensed the atmosphere in the same way that Rose had, he showed no sign of it, but after greeting the Vieillands he moved across to Kerry, and lifted her hand to his lips.

'Rose tells me you are engaged to marry this rascal here—' He gave Jacques a friendly thump on his shoulder. 'You'll have to keep him in order, you know.'

He spoke in French and Kerry looked at

him with wonder, not quite understanding, but catching the gist of his words. Then Philippe took Jacques' hand and shook it warmly.

'You're a lucky fellow to have found such a charming young lady willing to take you on.'

Monsieur Vieilland fetched a bottle from a cupboard, obviously reserved for special guests and offered drinks to Rose and Philippe. Rose refused politely, but Philippe accepted.

'Yes, indeed. This is a happy occasion and we should drink to the good health and happiness of the young couple. You know, Jacques, there will always be a job for you with the firm when you finish in the army, in fact since you will have a wife and family to support we shall have to see that it is a position commensurate with your needs.'

'Thank you, Monsieur du Caine,' Jacques answered. 'I wish I could be here this autumn for the grape harvest, but by next year I shall have finished my National Service, and the sooner it's over the better.'

'I know how you feel. It's several years now since I did my military training,' Philippe gave a dry laugh. 'It makes a man of you, so they say—I don't know about that, but it seems to me that you have to make the best of it while you're there and then it can be a worthwhile experience.'

He sat down beside Madame Vieilland and smiled at her.

'My grandmother was English, you know, so you'll understand why I find it very pleasing that the connection between the two countries is to be continued.'

'But they're both so young, don't you think?' murmured Madame Vieilland.

'Young? Madame, forgive me for asking —but you also must have been very young when you married, you certainly don't look old enough to have a son in the army.'

Madame smiled and glanced at her husband, she was pleased with the compliment. 'It's true—I was only nineteen, but—'

'There you are, then,' Philippe left her no time to voice further doubts. 'And I don't believe there's a happier couple in the whole of France. Let us drink a toast to you both for having made such a successful match.'

The conversation grew pleasanter and happier, the faces began to smile, soon laughter was ringing out in the room. Rose could not help noticing the respect that was accorded to Philippe, nor how somehow everything he said was carefully tuned to making them feel that this precipitate wedding was a blessing that had befallen them. Quietly, subtly, without in any way appearing to dictate, it soon became apparent that his position and his words carried great weight with Jacques' parents. He went out of his way to show pleasure at the match and therefore they felt it could not be as disastrous as they had evidently been imagining. As it was already late, they stayed for little over an hour. Philippe left at the same time as the girls and Jacques walked with them to the villa.

Rose went in and put on the kettle to make a cup of instant coffee and Kerry, after saying a lingering goodbye to Jacques, came in and joined her.

'That was a stroke of genius on your part to bring Philippe du Caine along. It made all the difference, it was terrible before then—honestly! I couldn't understand half that was being said, but I know most of it was pretty uncomplimentary. I felt like running away and Jacques was talking about leaving for good, and then you walked in—and they were eating out of that man's hand. I couldn't believe it—the difference it made! Thank you, Rose.'

'Don't thank me,' said Rose. 'I didn't actually invite him along.'

'Maybe, but he came because of you.'

'He was merely being polite, his aunt insisted that he should walk me to the house.'

'He seemed to know there was trouble the moment he walked in,' commented Kerry.

'That's not surprising. You could have cut the atmosphere with a knife. You all looked on the verge of tears.'

'I was. It was a disaster—but now I feel it's going to be all right. His father actually kissed me goodnight—that was a good sign, wasn't it?'

'I should say so.'

'You know, I believe Philippe did that for your sake—because I'm your friend,' Kerry mused.

'No, it couldn't possibly have been that,' said Rose. 'It's more likely that he guessed he might lose Jacques, and he didn't want that. In fact he said he'd give Jacques promotion when he comes out of the army. It's the sort of family business that

91

takes a paternalistic attitude.'

'Jacques is good at his job, I know that, but there was something else. I still believe it was also because Philippe thinks highly of you.'

Rose yawned. She knew such an idea was preposterous, but it was too late to sit up and discuss it further.

CHAPTER FOUR

Jacques' leave was only for seventy-two hours and he soon had to return to his unit, but by that time arrangements had been made for the wedding to take place in three weeks' time. Kerry had telephoned her parents to tell them of the date, but her news had been received with stony displeasure. They made no offer to attend or to help with arrangements in any way. Though Kerry wept when she told Rose about it, it made no difference to her determination to go ahead, and the girls decided they must make the best of a bad job.

As she had arranged with Miss Grantchester, Rose went to the Château every morning and spent a couple of hours helping her with correspondence and reading to her. When she arrived Yvette, the maid, would meet her in the hallway and escort her up the wide stairway to the suite of rooms that the old lady occupied. They were in the south wing where she got the maximum of sunlight which enabled her to see vaguely. Rose soon learned that every piece of furniture must be carefully left in its usual position; Miss Grantchester seemed to carry a map of it in her head which enabled her to negotiate chairs, tables, etc, easily and to remember where her typewriter was and her tapes. She very much enjoyed the talking books which were sent to her from England and spent a great deal of time listening to the radio in either English or French with equal ease.

Her grasp of business affairs was as clear as that of someone much younger, and if Rose had been in any doubt of the importance of the old lady's position, it was soon dispelled as she helped Miss Grantchester with letters, read Stock Exchange reports and dealt with numerous financial queries. Miss Grantchester was undoubtedly a very rich and powerful old lady. She was also Honorary President of several charitable organisations and though she could no longer attend meetings, she sent generous cheques to a number of worthy causes.

'It's been an absolute godsend, having you to help me,' she told Rose on more than one occasion.

Rose was happy to be of assistance and the work was varied and interesting; besides, the 'office' conditions were a dream. Miss Grantchester's rooms were the most beautiful Rose had ever seen. Spacious and graciously proportioned, they opened to a balcony which overlooked the lawns and swimming pool, petunias and geraniums made a riot of colour around the stone balustrade. When the sun was too hot to sit on the balcony they retired into the drawing-room and closed the slatted shutters and Rose worked at a large, highly polished antique desk. There were a couple of settees, some easy chairs and occasional tables, fresh flowers, usually delicately scented, and indeed though the room served as an office it was in the main a luxurious and very large lounge with one end set aside as a work area, adjoining it were Miss Grantchester's bedroom and luxurious bathroom. If she wanted anything she had only to ring and one of the maids, usually Yvette, appeared and her commands were carried out with the minimum of delay.

Usually Philippe was away on some business activity before Rose arrived at the Château and she had left long before he returned. It was not until the end of the week that she saw him. She had taken her leave as usual of Miss Grantchester, arranging to call in again on Monday morning. Rose was descending the stairs to let herself out when she encountered Philippe. He stood at that point where the stairs divided, beside the Grecian statue, and in the arrogant stance, the proudly held head, the aquiline nose there was a resemblance. Philippe could almost have modelled for the figure—except that he was clad in another lightweight business suit, this time of a blue-grey colour.

'Good morning, Rose. Would you step into my office for a moment.'

It was more of a command than a question. He stood to one side and fell into step beside her so that they descended the wide staircase together.

'This way.'

He crossed the hall with long athletic strides and opened a door for her to enter. Rose stepped into a very masculine study—like all the rooms in the Château it was large, well lit with perfectly proportioned windows, the walls were lined with bookshelves and there were half a dozen comfortable leather-upholstered armchairs. There was an imposing desk and behind it a well used swivel chair. At the far end was a large carved fireplace with a tapestry firescreen in front of the empty grate, and above the mantelpiece was an oil painting of the Château which looked as if it might have been executed a couple of hundred years ago, judging by the attire of the people who wandered in the grounds and the horses and carriages approaching along the drive.

Philippe ushered her to one of the armchairs, talking as he did so. 'Rose, I am very grateful for the help you have been giving my aunt—she tells me you have been most useful to her.'

'It's been a pleasure,' Rose murmured.

He went to his desk and picked up a cheque that was lying there.

'We never came to any arrangement about remuneration for your services.'

'There's no need. I—I don't mind, I haven't anything else to do.'

'Nevertheless, I know that it is interrupting your holiday—it must surely leave you with less time for—sunbathing?'

A wry smile twisted one corner of his lips as he said those words and Rose felt the colour deepening in her cheeks, remembering all too vividly how she had opened her eyes to find him gazing down at her as she lay topless on the rocks. She looked at her feet, unable to answer him, and there was a small silence in the room. Then he spoke, quite matter-of-factly.

'I've written out a cheque for you.'

'Really, I didn't expect to be paid,' she demurred.

'Nevertheless I think that some small remuneration will not come amiss, and I prefer that the arrangement should be on a business basis.'

He pushed the cheque into her reluctant hand. Rose glanced at the amount, did a rapid calculation to convert francs into pounds and tried to give it back to him.

'That's far too much, Monsieur du Caine. I haven't earned such a sum.'

He shrugged, dismissing it lightly. 'My aunt is well satisfied to have you here every morning. It gives me pleasure to see that she is happy and for my part it is a small price to pay for that. I should not like you to find yourself forced to leave her because of any financial difficulties.'

'But, Monsieur du Caine, I really hadn't thought of this as a regular job. I've been helping Miss Grantchester because it was useful to her and filled in my time. In any case, I shall only stay here until after the wedding.'

'I understood you had no job in Britain?'

'That's true, but—'

'Then there is no reason for you to leave, even after Kerry and Jacques are married, is there?'

'No—'

'I attach no strings. You will remain completely free and I know my aunt will be delighted to have your help for just as long as you are willing to give it. You say you find the work pleasant?'

'I do indeed.'

'Let us leave it at that. You will receive that amount each week for as long as you continue to work for my aunt. Rose, do not be too proud to take it,' he urged. 'Believe me, I am a businessman, I do not make deals unless they are to my advantage. If in this instance it helps you too, that is all to the good.'

There was no doubt that the money would come in useful. Paying for the repairs to the car had taken several of Rose's traveller's cheques, and though so far Kerry had generously paid for all their housekeeping expenses, she preferred to be independent.

'Thank you, Monsieur du Caine. I would have done my best for Miss Grantchester in any case—'

He inclined his head. 'You have already proved that. But that's enough of the Monsieur du Caine—you must know by now that my name is Philippe.'

'I do, but I've never been accustomed to calling my employers by their christian names.'

'Then it is high time you started. I have been calling you Rose for some time now. Try it.'

'Yes, Philippe,' she smiled.

'That's better.'

Rose had an uneasy feeling that she had been manipulated—pressurised into a commitment that would now be more binding than before—yet she liked working for Miss Grantchester and the money would indeed be useful. Generous though the sum seemed to Rose it was less than peanuts to the du Caines, so why should she have this uneasy feeling?

'I'd better be going now.'

She assumed that he would be quite ready to allow her to make her departure. He held open the door for her to walk through into the hall, then he asked, 'Has anyone shown you over the Château?'

'No, not really. I know Miss Grantchester's suite and I've been in the drawing-room and the dining-room and now your study, but that's all.'

'Come, I'll take you on a conducted tour.'

She hesitated, but Philippe was already moving towards a door which he held for her. They came into a long gallery, furnished with chaise-longues which stood between the pairs of Georgian windows. On the opposite wall were portraits of lovely ladies in elegant ball gowns, regal with ermine capes, and handsome men in colourful military uniforms.

'Are they ancestors of yours?' Rose asked.

'They are. Formidable-looking lot, don't you think?'

'I—I don't know. He's a bit like you.' She pointed to a lifesize painting at the far end of the gallery.

'I take that as a compliment. He's probably the best of the lot, for it was he who really expanded the company and he did most of the alterations to the house in the eighteenth century. He was lucky to escape with his head during the Revolution, but somehow he did, and increased the family fortunes to boot.'

He guided her through a huge pair of double doors and they were standing in a ballroom. It was panelled with painted wood of a delicate shade of pastel green, lined in cream and gold, but its most striking feature was the moulded ceiling with a large central painting of shepherdesses and cupids. Huge mirrors in gilt frames were placed at intervals around the walls and three beautiful crystal chandeliers hung from the ceiling.

'Do you use this often?' Rose asked, awestruck by the magnificence of the room.

'Very seldom. In fact I think it has not held a full-scale function since my twenty-first birthday, and that was ten years ago.'

101

'It must have been wonderful!'

'It was quite an event, but as with all the important happenings in this house I believe it was used more to entertain those who could be useful in the business than it was for my enjoyment,' Philippe smiled wryly. 'I was being introduced to all the important businessmen with whom I would soon have contact and it was done with the specific idea of making sure that I knew the right people, and what is more, that they were aware of the importance of the du Caines.'

'So you didn't enjoy it?'

'On the contrary, I enjoyed it immensely. It served its function precisely and I was launched on my career with the firm.'

Rose was not sure whether he meant to sound as coolly calculating as he did.

'But don't you sometimes have a party here—just for the fun of it?' she asked.

'Not that I can remember. If I wanted to have fun, I would arrange a party in one of the hotels or somewhere other than at the Château.'

She remembered how he often went into Les Virages and how Miss Grantchester disapproved of his visits there, and felt that perhaps she should not pursue that

102

subject further.

'Perhaps we will offer it to Jacques and Kerry for their wedding reception—do you think they would like that?'

'Really?' At first she thought he must be joking. 'You don't mean it, do you?'

He shrugged. 'Why not? It lies here empty—as you say, it is a waste not to use it. Of course I would expect them to make all the arrangements, I would not wish to be bothered with any details.'

She gazed at him with shining eyes. 'Oh, wait till I tell Kerry!'

'Before you do that, let me finish your tour of the house.'

Rose followed him, looking into various smaller rooms, including what he described as the schoolroom, where he had been taught by a tutor until he was old enough to attend his English public school, and the nursery suite that opened off it. Then they came to a lovely set of apartments on the first floor, on the opposite side of the landing to those of Miss Grantchester and nearer the head of the stairs.

'These were my grandmother's rooms,' Philippe remarked. 'That's a rather good portrait of her.'

The lady in the portrait wore a lacy

gown, straight-waisted but with a pointed hemline at mid-calf, a style of the 1920s. She was adorned with long strings of beautiful beads, a golden bangle on her shapely arm, and she was stunningly beautiful. Her hair, was immaculately bobbed, curved in a soft curl around one shell-like ear, there was a touch of irrepressible gaiety in the half smile that curved her lips and her stance showed grace and suppleness, such delicate loveliness that by comparison Rose felt plain and awkward. The women in Philippe's family had all been outstanding—his mother, Miss Grantchester, and now this gorgeous grandmother who smiled so serenely from the portrait—how wonderful it must be to look like that!

'My room is through there—' he pointed to the adjoining door. 'It used to be my grandfather's, of course. This room has been empty since my grandmother died.'

They walked out to the landing.

'Would you like to see the battlements? There should be a good view on a bright day like this.'

As usual he did not wait for her assent but took it for granted and led the way down a long corridor to the door at the

104

end. It opened to a circular stairway, obviously in one of the turrets of the Château.

'There are quite a lot of steps, but I think you'll find it rewarding when we get there. It's a bit dark, so I'll lead the way.'

As he mounted the steps he took hold of Rose's hand, guiding her up behind him. Gradually her eyes became accustomed to the lack of light—it was not completely dark, there were slits of windows at intervals but in between the light was dim. She stumbled and Philippe's grip on her hand tightened, she could feel the muscles of his arm tauten to hold her and his strength was such that she felt perfect confidence.

He knew exactly where he was going, knew every twist and turn of the old circular stairway. It was not lack of trust that made her knees slightly wobbly, it was the effect of that grip on her hand, the pressure of his fingers, the fact that when he stopped to allow her to come up to the step behind him her body brushed against his legs. Her heartbeat was quickened, but immediately he moved on again.

It was a relief when they came to the

top of the flight of steps. Philippe let go of her hand and pulled aside a heavy bolt on a trapdoor, it opened to let in the hot bright sunshine, and she felt warm air fan her cheek. Philippe stepped out, fastened the door, then leaned down to take her hand once more and Rose emerged to stand beside him. They were on a circular stone walkway around the turret top. There was a narrow gulley close to the battlemented wall and in the centre was a conical slate-covered roof, surprisingly large now that they were standing beside it, a shape that gave the Château its fanciful, almost fairytale appearance.

The wind whipped Rose's hair as she stepped forward to look over the battlements and she gasped with delight as her eyes swept over the wide countryside. The view was breathtaking; the plain immediately below stretched away, thick with vines, dotted with small villages, clustered roofs of higgledy-piggledy houses turned rose-pink in the sunshine. The river snaked through the greenery and roads marched with military precision towards the distance where a range of mountains turned the horizon into a muted, jagged mauve-coloured mist. Above the sky shone brilliantly blue.

'It's superb!' Rose exclaimed. 'You can see for miles!'

Philippe looked pleased at her enthusiasm.

'Yes. I have seen it clearer, but it's not too bad. That's Les Virages.' He pointed to the town Rose had been looking towards.

'It seems close enough from here. I reckon I could have walked it,' she laughed.

'You came pretty near to doing so,' Philippe said briefly. 'Come round the other side, you can get a bird's eye view of Chandelle. I'll show you where you live.'

He took hold of her hand again, eager as a boy to show her the beauties of his Château. Rose followed willingly enough to another viewpoint where he halted and put a hand on her shoulder to point through the trees to a corner of roof.

'That's Ste Thérèse, I think.'

Rose followed his pointing finger, noticed the church standing beside the small square and then, close to it, the villa. She even recognised her own bikini hanging on the line at the side of the house but she kept quiet about that.

'Yes, that's it. You get a lovely view of the church too, and there's the river again.'

'That's right. It loops around the Château, it made the place a natural fortress, and this height gave excellent viewpoints on all sides to complete its defence. You can't quite see our swimming place from here because it is hidden by the trees and the rocks. Beyond that the river sweeps away southwards—eventually it flows into the Mediterranean. You can drive there and back in a day, though it's quite a long trip—better to stay overnight. We'll do it some time, if you like.'

Rose felt warning signals. What was he suggesting? She knew she must be careful of this man, he could easily exert too great an influence on her. She turned to go back to the trapdoor, but as she did so a sudden stronger gust of wind caught her, swinging her momentarily off balance, and she swayed towards Philippe. His arms were there ready—she was caught once again in his embrace.

'I'm sorry. It was the wind—I—I didn't mean—'

His face was close to hers, he was looking down at her with a mocking smile.

'Didn't mean what?'

He made no attempt to kiss her, though something perverse in her longed that he should do so, despite the fact that she was vigorously pushing herself away from him.

'I didn't mean to throw myself into your arms,' she answered with an attempt at lightness.

'I had deduced that,' he replied, but there was no humour in his voice. 'I have not forgotten that day at the river—but don't make it too hard for me, Rose.'

'I—I don't know what you mean.'

'You don't?'

He stepped back as he spoke so that he was holding her at arm's length and his dark, beautiful eyes raked over her face, making her so very aware of his magnetic physical attraction. He seemed to be making a calculating assessment, to be trying to read something from her face, from her expression and the way he looked at her was deeply disturbing. His eyes lingered on her mouth, her lips had been slightly parted and instinctively she

109

closed them firmly. Philippe gave a light mocking laugh and then his gaze lifted so that his eyes stared directly into hers, and that was more than she could bear. Her lids dropped to shield her thoughts from him.

'I—I think I'd better go,' she stammered. 'It—it must be getting late—'

'You don't trust me, do you, Rose?'

His question was a challenge. How could she answer it? To admit it was true might sound insulting and would acknowledge how vulnerable she felt when she was with him. To deny it would be so blatantly untrue, yet it was not so much him that she did not trust, it was the effect he had on her. Though still unable to look at him she met his question with another.

'I—I don't know. Should I?'

He did not answer immediately but lightly brushed the softness of her cheek with the back of one finger. It was a gesture he might have made to a child, and as at their first meeting Rose felt a resentment stirring, feeling that he was refusing to treat her as an adult. But his words jolted her.

'Yes, Rose, you may trust me. We du Caines may find it very hard to resist trying to make love to a beautiful woman, but never, never would we respond to the challenge of desire by force. Does that make you feel safer?'

She looked at him then and there was that mocking glint in his eyes again. Once again he was simply teasing her—that was obvious when he referred to a beautiful woman. Rose had no illusions as to whether she merited being so classified! There was nothing really disproportionate about any of her features—but beauty! That was another matter entirely.

'Now you're laughing at me,' she said.

'On the contrary, I assure you, I meant every word. Come, let us go down.'

So he indicated that the conversation as well as the tour of the Château was ended. A few minutes later they were back in the main hallway, he opened the outer door for her, with casual friendliness he shook her hand and Rose walked out.

Kerry was out when Rose arrived back at the villa. She went through to her room and flung her handbag down on the bed, then crossed to the dressing-table and stood staring at her reflection in the mirror. Philippe's words were so fresh in her memory that he might almost have

111

been there in the room speaking them afresh.

'We du Caines may find it very hard to resist trying to make love to a beautiful woman—'

Rose heaved a sigh. It was just a pleasant turn of phrase, a touch of French charm. She pushed back a lock of fair hair that had fallen over her forehead, shading her candid blue eyes. She touched her cheek where Philippe's finger had brushed it—true, the skin was soft and glowed with health, it was getting quite becomingly tanned too—but beautiful? No. Never in her most optimistic mood could she have accepted that! She was just a pleasant-looking English girl, with a young face too rounded for beauty; her figure was too plump, she knew that, and her mouth was probably a little too generous. No, that phrase had not been the important one of the words Philippe had spoken to her. In fact when she analysed it, perhaps he was even suggesting, in the kindest way he could, that she could never mean anything to him. Yes, undoubtedly that had been the real import—that he admitted himself to be a flirt, that women in general were attractive to him, that he was always willing to respond to the challenge—but did she present a challenge to him? Ridiculous! She must not think about it any more. She moved away from the mirror, deciding there was no consolation in staring at her own reflected image any longer.

'Rose?'

Kerry was back, her arms laden with groceries. Rose joined her friend in the kitchen and together they prepared a skimpy meal. They usually ate little at lunchtime, preferring to make a more substantial meal in the evening.

'I've been looking through my wardrobe,' said Kerry. 'I can't think what I'm going to wear for the wedding. I haven't got a thing that's suitable. Dad left me some money, but that was only to pay for day-to-day living—I never thought of the expense of a wedding, and I can't just let Jacques and his parents pay for everything.'

Rose opened her handbag and took out the cheque that Philippe had given her.

'Here you are. It's not a great deal, but I've paid nothing for my keep till now.'

'I can't take that, Rose,' protested Kerry. 'It's yours. You don't owe me a thing—honestly, I didn't mean—'

'I know you didn't. But I didn't expect

to get this anyway. I would have refused it, but Philippe was insistent.'

'So he should be, the du Caines can well afford it.'

'Okay, then let's use it to buy you a wedding dress. If we had a sewing machine we could get material and make something up ourselves, and it'd be cheaper.'

Kerry's eyes brightened. 'Madame Vieilland has one. I saw it when I was up at the house. A lovely modern electric machine—and you're so clever at making clothes, would you do it for me, Rose?'

'I'd love to. You see if we can borrow the machine and then we'll go into Les Virages and get some material.'

The loan of the sewing machine was easily arranged. Madame Vieilland was really quite pleased to think that her future daughter-in-law was able to do her own dressmaking, and Kerry omitted to tell her that it would be Rose who would do the main part of the work. The following afternoon the girls set out in the little green Mini to buy materials and patterns, determined to make the small amount of money stretch as far as possible.

There were some good shops in Les

Virages, and though Kerry lingered momentarily looking in one of the windows at a very elegant and wildly expensive wedding gown of Chantilly lace, she soon brushed such dreams from her mind when she looked at the price tag. Rose admired the cheerful acceptance that Kerry displayed, knowing that she had been used to living at a very comfortable standard. Mr Langham had always had a much better paid job than had Rose's father and after they moved away from the district his promotion had put them in a different financial league altogether—Kerry would have had a really super wedding if she had not had this terrible rift with her parents. Nevertheless she was cheerfully accepting things as they were and her love for Jacques was so strong that she made light of all difficulties. Looking at her, Rose thought, You're beautiful, Kerry, I can well see how Jacques fell in love with you.

'I think I'd like quite a simple style really,' said Kerry.

'Let's see if they've got some pattern books, then,' Rose suggested.

Soon the girls were poring through the pages. They took their time in deciding. Kerry's idea of a simple dress was a

Victorian style with elaborate tucks around the bodice and a high frilled neckline, but Rose agreed that it would suit her admirably. It would take several hours of painstaking work, but the materials need not be too expensive which was what they were aiming at. For her bridesmaid's dress Rose chose a similar type of gown, but much simpler in style and a delightful shade of apple green.

The two girls were chatting excitedly as they left the shop and walked down the street towards where the Mini was parked. They waited to cross the road; a car was approaching, and at once Rose recognised it—the low very dark blue sports car that belonged to Philippe du Caine. She stood as if mesmerised, not wanting to look closely yet unable to take her eyes away. Kerry noticed it too.

'Look, there's Philippe du Caine—and see who he's got with him! Wow-ee!'

Rose had seen all too clearly the bouncing dark hair of a lovely girl; she caught a glimpse of sophisticated dark glasses, a brightly coloured dress and a mouth wide open as the girl laughed with evident *joie-de-vivre*. Again those words of his snapped into Rose's mind. *We du*

116

Caines may not be able to resist trying to make love to a beautiful woman—Rose felt an unreasoning stab of jealousy. She turned to Kerry.

'Who is it, do you know?'

'No. Must be *the woman*,' Kerry hinted darkly. 'You know—the one he's always visiting, I told you he's always in the news being about with some glamorous female. Don't think I've seen that one before.' She shrugged. 'But that's how it is with him. Come on, we can cross now.'

Kerry put Philippe and the girl out of her mind immediately, but Rose found it difficult to do so. She wished she did not care, tried to make herself believe that in truth it was of no concern to her, but the effort was hollow. She had never in her life met anyone so exciting and charming as Philippe du Caine. She knew he could be pleasant and that on occasions he was kind and thoughtful, that he was a powerful businessman, capable of thinking big and making far-reaching decisions, yet always at the back of her mind was this feeling that he was not quite respectable, especially in his dealings with women. The girl in the car had been older than Rose—not old by any means, but with just those few more years that gave self-confidence, poise, sophistication, all those qualities that she felt sure Philippe must admire and which she was so conscious of lacking herself.

'Rose—this way.' Kerry tugged at her arm.

Rose smiled at her friend. What a fool she was to spend so much time in thinking about him. The sooner she put Philippe du Caine out of her mind the better—she ought to be glad she had seen him this afternoon with his beautiful companion, it would help her to put any silly ideas concerning him out of her head. She made herself concentrate on the sewing she was about to undertake.

'I reckon I could get your dress cut out and pinned tonight,' she told Kerry with determination.

CHAPTER FIVE

The days simply flew by, there was so much to do. Rose continued to spend every morning with Miss Grantchester and most afternoons she was sewing and helping Kerry with other preparations. Miss Grantchester took a great interest in all the proceedings, delighted in Rose's descriptions of the dresses she was making, so Rose took pieces of the materials for the old lady to feel.

'I shall be able to imagine exactly how you both look at the wedding,' she exclaimed. 'This is a totally unexpected joy for me.'

She meant what she said. The involvement of the du Caines had certainly made a difference in the attitude of Jacques' family too. They were quite overwhelmed to think that for the reception, though it was not to be a large gathering, they could use the grand ballroom of the Château.

At last the wedding dress was finished—and Rose was well pleased with the result. Kerry would be a beautiful bride in the gown she had made with such care, the attention she had given to the detail was well worth the extra trouble and it fitted her perfectly. Her own dress was quietly becoming; it was full length with a frill around the hem, and economically Rose felt she would be able to make use of it later for informal evening wear.

Then Kerry and Rose began to plan

refreshments for the reception, and this time they were close to despair. Kerry had sent to England to withdraw the little money she had in the savings bank, but even so there was far too little to buy delicacies and even if they made things, the ingredients would be expensive. Jacques' parents came from large families and all the cousins and aunts and uncles would be descending on Chandelle for the wedding. But quite unexpectedly there came a letter from Kerry's mother.

Rose was clearing away the breakfast things when the postman called. Kerry left the envelope in her mother's handwriting on the table and curled up to enjoy a long, loving letter from Jacques. She was still reading it when Rose left for her morning at the Château. It was not until she returned at lunch time that she learned the good news.

'They're coming to the wedding after all,' Kerry beamed. 'And look at this!'

She placed a cheque on the table; it was for a substantial sum of money, signed by Mr Langham. Rose could hardly believe it. Mr and Mrs Langham had been so adamant that they would have nothing to do with the wedding, always insisting that Kerry should return home, that there was no need for her to have the baby, or that she could have it adopted. Suddenly, it seemed, they had had a change of heart, they must have realised that if they persisted in their refusal they would lose their daughter for good.

'It's not only Mummy and Daddy who're coming, but my brother and his wife and their two children. The whole family will be here!' Kerry's eyes were shining. 'I'm so excited! I was happy before, of course, but this makes all the difference. I hated going against their wishes, but nothing would make me give up Jacques.'

'You proved that,' Rose smiled.

'And look at the size of that cheque! Wow-ee! Now I won't feel like a Cinderella at my own wedding, we'll really be able to lay on the works now.'

'It was certainly very generous of your father—but shouldn't you perhaps put a little of it aside for the future?' Rose suggested.

'Why should I?' Kerry grinned. 'Jacques and I were going to manage without it before, weren't we?'

'Yes, but—'

'None of your buts, Rose. I'm going to

121

have just the sort of wedding I always dreamed about.'

Rose smiled. Despite her suggestions of caution she couldn't really blame Kerry and she was delighted to see her friend's happiness. Besides, it would certainly lift a lot of the problems she had been worrying about.

'Daddy says no doubt I'll want to buy a wedding dress,' Kerry laughed.

'Perhaps you should—'

'Not on your life! Nothing could be prettier than the one you've made me. I wouldn't change that if I was a millionaire.' Kerry gave Rose a hug. 'But we'll find the name of a local caterers and order whatever they usually provide for a wedding feast. Incidentally, we don't have to worry about drinks because Jacques tells me that the du Caines have offered to provide all the wine we need from their stocks. Isn't that marvellous?'

So the days sped by and the wedding day came nearer and nearer. The imminent arrival of Kerry's family presented one more problem—how were they all to be fitted into the tiny villa? It was Miss Grantchester who first broached this subject to Rose when she told the old lady how many would be arriving.

'How will you manage to sleep them all?' she asked.

'I'm sure we'll all fit in somehow,' Rose laughed. 'I can always sleep on the floor—it won't be the first time I've done that.'

'You'll do no such thing,' declared Miss Grantchester. 'We have plenty of rooms here at the Château. You'll come up here to stay.'

Rose hesitated. She knew that it would relieve the congestion at the villa if she accepted, but she was reluctant to do so. She had seen little of Philippe during the past week or so and on the few occasions when they had encountered one another he had been friendly, but she had felt a certain remoteness in him. Miss Grantchester as usual, however, took Rose's consent for granted.

'I'll tell the servants to prepare a room.'

So it was arranged. Kerry's family were due to arrive on the eve of the wedding and on that evening Rose prepared to sleep at the Château. But there was a surprise in store for her when she returned to the villa at lunch time, for there sitting at the kitchen table was—Charles, her boy-friend!

She stared at him in astonishment.

'I bet you're surprised to see me.' He stood up as she entered and walked towards her. His arms encircled her and he gave her a bear-like hug and a kiss.

'Charles! I—I thought you'd gone to Greece or somewhere.'

'I did. I've been around—I've got so much to tell you. Marvellous time.'

'But how did you get here?'

'Hitched. I rang your home, hoping to have a word with you, and your mother gave me this address. Aren't you pleased to see me?'

'Yes. Yes, of course. You've got thinner.'

Rose stood back and surveyed him critically as he released her. His hair was too long, unkempt-looking, his face thin and drawn despite the tan of living mainly in the open air. He slumped down into a chair again.

'Are you tired?' she asked solicitously.

He nodded. 'Haven't had much rest lately. I ran short of money and cut down on food—things are so much more expensive than I expected. And I had my camera stolen. That was really why I phoned you, I was going to ask you if you could arrange to send me some

124

money—just a loan, of course—but when I heard you were here well, I just had to potter along and see you.'

'Poor Charles!'

'Not at all,' he said sharply. 'I've had a great time. Wait till I've had something to eat and caught up on my sleep, then I'll tell you all about it.'

'When did you get here?' she asked.

'Only about ten minutes ago. I was just having a cup of coffee with Kerry.'

'Have we anything for lunch?' Rose asked her friend.

She was troubled to see Charles looking so pale and thin. He had always been so robust, a star of the football team, full of life and energy.

'Not much,' Kerry admitted. 'I thought we'd just have our usual cheese and salad and fruit.'

Rose glanced at the alarm clock that stood on the dresser.

'I'll dash down to the village and see what I can get,' she said. 'There's just time before they close for the afternoon siesta.'

Charles stood up again. 'I'll come with you.'

'No need—you stay here and have a rest—'

He had already moved towards the door and held it open for Rose.

'Now you're clucking at me like a mother hen! That's not how I think of you, Rose. Come on, let's see what delectables they have on offer in this backwater.'

Kerry said, 'I'll peel a few potatoes while you're away.'

As they hurried along the path and down into the village street Charles put his arm fondly around Rose's waist.

'You're looking absolutely great, Rose. Life here seems to suit you.'

'Why, thank you, Charles.' She was a little surprised that he had noticed. He always seemed to have taken her so much for granted before. 'I wish I could say the same about you.'

'Don't keep rubbing it in,' he protested. 'You wait till I tell you the things that have happened to yours truly. It'll fairly make your hair stand on end—it's a wonder I'm alive to tell the tale!'

'Really?'

She remembered he had always had a propensity for exaggeration and was not sure how much truth there would be in his stories. His grip on her waist tightened and he pulled her closer towards him.

'Give us a kiss, Rose.'

He attempted to take her in his arms, and although there was no one else in the street just then, Rose felt embarrassed.

'Not here, Charles. Besides, we've got to hurry.'

'Just one little kiss, darling—'

Rose heard the car approaching before she saw it. She seized on it as an excuse, trying to wrest herself from his hold as she moved towards the side of the road. Charles had also heard the car and his response was the same as hers, only he still held her close, in fact as Rose came to the old brick wall she found herself pinioned against it by him.

'Charles—'

It was impossible to escape now, the street was narrow and the car passed within a few feet as Charles bent his head to take that kiss. Rose saw it and recognised it, a very dark blue powerful sports model. As it cruised past at the moderate speed that was necessary to negotiate safely through the village, she not only recognised the car, she also recognised the driver, and with a feeling of acute embarrassment knew that Philippe had seen her too. A moment later she felt the dry hard pressure of Charles'

127

lips on hers. She was also aware that he had obviously not been able to get his clothes washed recently, and she resolved to do something about that as soon as possible. Though his kiss in no way roused her, she still felt responsible for him in a curious detached way. Perhaps it was because he seemed such a boy compared with Philippe—

She stopped herself as that thought flashed into her mind, Philippe meant nothing to her, nor she to him—he enjoyed teasing her, found her lightly amusing, but that was all there was to it. There was no reason why she should feel so acutely embarrassed because he had seen her in the arms of Charles, but the fact remained that she was. Try as she might to stop thinking about Philippe he had begun to dominate her in a way that troubled her deeply. Charles released her as suddenly as he had seized her. He was looking at her with an odd expression.

'Hey, Rose, penny for your thoughts! You weren't with me at all.'

His voice held reproach. Rose shrugged; her thoughts were far too complicated to explain even if she had wanted to—besides, she couldn't even understand them herself.

It was as if she was in the grip of some super-power—magical, mysterious, disturbing. It made her angry with herself, and to overcome this she began to walk swiftly down the street.

'Come on, Charles. Once the butcher closes, he's shut for at least three hours, from one o'clock till four.'

Charles fell into step beside her and they reached the shop just as the butcher, resplendent in white coat and straw hat, was about to lock the door. For a moment he looked as if he would signal that they were too late, then he recognised Rose.

'It's the young lady from the Château, isn't it?'

Rose was surprised. 'Er—yes, I do help Miss Grantchester—'

'I've heard about you from my niece. You know her? Yvette?'

'Why, of course. I see her almost every day.'

The butcher nodded vigorously. 'Won't be long now to the wedding. Jacques is a great favourite in the village, I reckon there'll be a good turn-out to see him married.'

Rose had not realised that she and Kerry had become so well known in the village.

Probably it should have been obvious, for in the small town where she lived in England, it was just the same, any stranger would be noticed and discussed and fitted into some category, yet she had never envisaged the same thing happening in Chandelle. That day she had cause to be grateful that it was so. If she had been a passing stranger the butcher's shop would have been closed to her; as it was, being a fellow-employee at the Château with the butcher's niece gave her the right to preferential treatment. On his recommendation she bought cutlets of best quality pork, tender and lean.

After the meal Charles readily accepted Rose's proposal that he should take a sleep and give her his dirty clothes to wash. He insisted on using the bedroll he had carried with him throughout his trip so as not to disturb the arrangements Rose and Kerry had made ready for the Langham family's arrival. Kerry also took a brief nap, while Rose busied herself at the sink with detergents and a scrubbing brush, as there was no washing machine. Soon she had a line of garments hanging out in the bright sun and reflected how much easier it was to cope with washing where you could rely on a good dry day. In England one had so often to keep running in and out to fetch in half dried clothes as showers of rain threatened to wet them all again.

Nevertheless by the time she had pressed and folded the last of the pile that had been extracted from Charles's rucksack, she was beginning to feel quite tired. It seemed as if he had not had a single clean item left in it, but there was a satisfaction in placing the fresh clothes on the chair beside him when they were ready. Charles continued to sleep soundly.

'Better leave him there,' Kerry suggested when she wandered in, yawning. 'Heavens, just look at the time! What'll we give the family for dinner tonight, Rose?'

'I don't know. I thought you would have planned that.'

'I forgot. Anyway, perhaps Daddy'll take us all down to the restaurant in the village.'

'I don't think we should expect that,' said Rose. 'Besides, the children will be too tired to go out after their long journey.'

'I suppose you're right,' Kerry agreed reluctantly. 'But there'll be nine of us! Whatever can we do?'

'Let's make a good thick vegetable soup

for a start,' Rose suggested. 'We'll get some freshly baked bread to go with it and then a selection of cooked meats, salad stuffs and things from the charcuterie.'

'Okay,' Kerry agreed readily. 'And we can have fresh fruit and cream and biscuits and cheeses for dessert. We'll need more coffee too.'

Together they made out a shopping list and went once again to the village, where the shops were open from four o'clock till seven. Though it was a small place the locals were as fastidious about food as anywhere else in France, and the shops carried an excellent selection of high-quality goods. It was non-stop work for the girls, but they worked with a will together—Kerry might have been loath to begin, but once she started she entered into it wholeheartedly. Their preparations were just about completed when the two cars drove up outside Ste Thérèse. Then the house was full of Langhams, Kerry was enveloped in loving kisses from her parents and from her brother and his wife and from her little niece and nephew. Having decided they must make the best of the situation they were evidently determined that there should be no reproaches, and though there were tears in Mrs Langham's eyes she hurriedly brushed them aside.

'Now then, Mummy, you're not to cry—I know mothers always do at weddings, but this is a happy occasion and I won't have it,' Kerry teased her.

'I know, my dear, I know,' her mother sighed.

'You haven't greeted Rose yet. She's been an absolute brick—I don't know how I would have managed without her,' said Kerry.

Mrs Langham gave Rose a hug and a kiss. 'I can believe that. It's so good to see you, Rose—and how well you're looking. France certainly suits you.'

So the merry chatter went on.

'Did you have a good journey?'

'What are the arrangements for the wedding?'

'Jacques is coming home this evening.'

'Is there anything we can do?'

'Be quiet, stop teasing Lucy!'

'How are you feeling, Kerry?'

Charles woke up at last. They had begun the meal when he ambled into the kitchen looking sleepy and tousled but so much cleaner and fresher in blue jeans and a black tee-shirt stamped with a gold replica of the label from a stout bottle. Once again Rose thought how immature he looked, just a boy, not yet really having attained the stature of manhood, though with a swagger that was almost rough, he pretended that he had. He sat down and Rose served him with a large helping of soup, which everyone said was delicious.

The meal seemed to go on for a long time, mostly because there was so much to talk about as well as everyone being rather hungry. It was almost over when Jacques arrived, and that called for more introductions and greetings. He had come to invite them all up to his parents' house, so that they might all get acquainted before the wedding.

'It's getting late for the children,' Kerry's sister-in-law demurred.

'Not if we go now,' suggested her brother.

'You must all come,' Kerry insisted. 'I do so want Jacques' parents to meet you, then you won't be strangers tomorrow. You'll come too, won't you, Rose?'

'I don't think so. I'm a little tired and I don't want to be too late going up to the Château.'

So it was that Kerry and her family all

left with the table still piled with dirty dishes. Jacques said they would have coffee and liqueurs with his parents, so Rose sat down and poured mugs of coffee for herself and Charles. He reached out a hand and covered hers where it lay on the table, and instinctively she pulled away from his touch.

'I'd better get on with this washing up,' she excused herself.

'Leave it, Rose. Every time I try to come close to you, you move away.'

He walked round to where she sat and put his arms around her. His hand touched her breast beneath her open-necked shirt dress, and somehow it gave her a shrinking feeling. Instinctively her hands flew up to shield them covering the neck of her dress, which must have been gaping open a little too revealingly from where Charles stood behind her chair.

'Come off it, Rose—you didn't act like that last time we were together.'

That last time had been after the end-of-term dance. All the girls had been there with boy-friends and there had been quite a lot of kissing and petting. Then, it was true, she had welcomed his kisses, had wanted to be caressed by him—but now

135

somehow it was different; there was no excitement in being alone with Charles.

'I guess I'm just tired,' she excused herself.

'I hope that's all it is,' Charles grumbled. 'I've come a long way to see you.'

'I thought you came here because you'd run out of money,' she said flatly. She began to stack the dishes beside the sink.

'You know it wasn't just that. I really was keen to see you, Rose—but you seem to have changed.'

'Perhaps I have,' she shrugged. 'Anyway, I don't want to discuss it now. I'm going up to the Château tonight.'

'Why?'

'There's no spare room for me here, now that the family have arrived.'

'You can share my sleeping bag.'

'No, thank you.'

'I was only joking, Rose.' He looked crestfallen. 'Have you lost your sense of humour?'

'Sorry,' she sighed.

'If you're going to misinterpret everything I say or do, I guess I'd better get out of your way,' Charles said crossly. 'Goodnight.'

He walked out of the kitchen. Rose

made no attempt to stop him. She began to wash up. With nine of them for supper there was a big pile of dirty dishes, and it was sheer determination that made her carry on until all were cleaned. She drew the line at drying up and decided to leave them to drain, as it was already quite late. Then, collecting her suitcase, she put it into her little car and drove up to the Château.

It was very dark as she manoeuvred to park in an out-of-the-way corner of the courtyard. As she switched off the car lights the doors of the Château opened and a large figure stood framed in the doorway. It was Philippe, there was no mistaking that, with his height and the breadth of his shoulders silhouetted against the glow of the lights from the entrance. He was wearing a formal dinner jacket, and Rose noticed the athletic grace with which his figure narrowed to the hips—and then as she turned to pull out her suitcase he bounded down the steps.

'I'll take that.'

Matching action to words, he was beside her in seconds, and their hands touched as he took hold of the handle. Foolishly Rose wondered if he had been looking out for her, but his next words dispelled that idea. Anyway, it was obvious that he had been out to dinner, and there was a light whiff of good brandy on his breath.

'I left Aunt Celia's talking book in my car, I was just going to fetch it for her,' he said. 'You're late, Rose. The old lady was beginning to get worried about you.'

'There were one or two things to do at the villa,' Rose explained as she walked beside him towards the house. 'Kerry's parents arrived this evening, and her brother and his wife and their children.'

They were in the light of the doorway now.

'And the young man I saw you with at lunch time?' Philippe asked.

Rose found herself blushing and wished she was still outside in the darkness. Here in the brightly lit hallway the lights were far too revealing, but she was naturally candid and she answered truthfully.

'That was Charles Maybury. He—we used to go to school together.'

'I see.'

There was a wealth of meaning in those two words that was not lost on Rose. A moment later Philippe asked more directly.

'He's your boy-friend, I take it?'

'No.' Her answer came quickly—too quickly.

'I got the impression that you were, shall we say, on quite intimate terms?'

Philippe's voice was gentle, he spoke softly yet with a deliberation that insisted on finding out the truth.

'We—we hadn't seen each other for a long time,' Rose said.

Philippe inclined his head. 'Therefore it was perfectly natural that he should be eager to kiss his charming girl-friend.'

'I'm not his girl-friend,' Rose protested again. 'I've spent most of the evening telling him that. I really don't see why I should go over it all again with you. What does it matter to you anyway?'

Philippe's deep, dark eyes were unfathomable, but he clicked his heels together and gave her a slight mocking bow from the hips.

'Forgive me, my dear. I had no idea I was intruding upon such a touchy subject. I assure you I have not the least desire to know any more about it.' He waved his hand, indicating that she should move on. 'Let us go in and tell Aunt Celia that her guest has arrived.'

So he left Rose feeling foolishly that she had read more into his questions than he had intended, and emphasised the point that what she did was of no account to him by referring to her, not as *our* guest but as Aunt Celia's. Well, that was true. Yet still she had the feeling that there had been some hidden motive behind Philippe's questions.

Miss Grantchester turned towards them as soon as the door opened. Her alertness never ceased to surprise Rose; it was often difficult to remember that the old lady could not see her, nevertheless she made a point of speaking the moment she entered the room.

'Good evening, Miss Grantchester. I hope I haven't kept you up, there's been so much to do down at the villa.'

'That's all right, my dear, I quite understand. But I'm sure you must be tired, and you've got a big day tomorrow.'

'I think everything's ready, and now that Kerry's parents are here it should all be plain sailing. But I must admit I am a bit weary,' Rose confessed.

'Of course you are. Now is there anything you want before we show you up to your room? A hot drink and a biscuit, perhaps?'

'No, thank you, Miss Grantchester,' Rose replied. 'There's absolutely nothing I need.'

'Then, Philippe, if you would be good enough to ring for Yvette—'

He tugged the tasselled bell pull and in a few moments it was answered by the smiling maidservant.

'I'm ready for bed, now, Yvette,' said Miss Grantchester. 'We'll show Rose to her room as we go. Where did you put her suitcase, Philippe?'

'It's all right, *mademoiselle,*' said Yvette. 'I've already had it taken up to Mademoiselle Rose's room.'

Philippe crossed the room and helped his aunt to her feet. She looked a diminutive figure standing beside him, though she was only a little below average height for a woman. Gently he bent and kissed her once on each cheek. He escorted her to the door and then handed her arm to the maid, who led her to where she could rest her hand on the banister and find her way upstairs. There was no real need for him to have helped her at all and evidently it was simply a little courtesy

141

that expressed the strong bond of affection between them. Rose felt quite touched by their devotion. She followed them to the doorway. Philippe stepped through to allow space for her to pass, and she turned towards him with a smile.

'Goodnight, Philippe.'

She held out her hand to shake his in the usual formality, but taking it, he raised it to his lips and bending his head kissed it on the knuckles. It was not just a light brush of the lips—both the grasp of his fingers and the pressure of his lips were firm and positive, a strong contact that sent a tingling sensation up her arm and set her heartbeat quickening. It was a deliberately sensual gesture, and as he slowly lifted his head his eyes sought hers and she knew he was capable of assessing her reaction and there seemed to be a hint of satisfaction in the mocking smile he gave her. Then at last he released her hand.

'Goodnight, Rose.'

She turned and followed Miss Grantchester upstairs so quickly that she almost stumbled. Then she took a deep breath, lifted her head high and put all her effort into making the ascent in a calm manner. At the top she turned to glance back, but Philippe had already withdrawn again into the lounge. Miss Grantchester and Yvette waited for Rose by the door to her room. She stepped inside, then halted in confusion.

'But—but this room—it was Philippe's grandmother's!' she exclaimed.

'It was. Now for a few nights, it's yours,' said Miss Grantchester. 'I think you'll find it's very pleasant. It has a lovely view over the gardens and it has its own bathroom.'

'I—I—'

'Don't you like it, Rose?'

'Yes, it's perfectly beautiful. But I never expected you to take so much trouble just for me—anything would have done.'

'Silly girl! It was no more trouble to prepare this room than any other. Now have you got everything you need here? If not just ring and someone will come and see to you. Goodnight, my dear.'

'Goodnight, Miss Grantchester—and thank you so much.' Rose leaned forward and kissed the old lady. 'You're so kind.'

'Rubbish! Pleasure to have you,' Miss Grantchester dismissed her gratitude gruffly, but Rose could tell she was pleased. 'Come, Yvette, or we'll never get to bed tonight.'

They left and Rose closed the door behind them. She turned round and round, looking at the room with delight and wonder. Never had she slept anywhere so grand or so big or so beautiful. She looked into the bathroom and that too had an elegance that more than made up for the fact that it was old-fashioned, patterned blue and white tiling with a polished mahogany surround to the bath and the basin, and when she turned on the taps water spouted from the mouths of golden dolphins. It was inviting, but she felt too tired to take a bath just then.

Suddenly Rose remembered something else that Philippe had told her when he had taken her on that conducted tour of the house. He slept in the adjoining room that had been his grandfather's. She walked quickly out of the bathroom and searched for the communicating door. It was so skilfully set into the panelling of the room that at first she did not notice it—then she looked more carefully and discovered it almost at once. She moved across the room and turned the handle. It opened silently. Without looking any farther she slammed it shut again and searched for a key or a bolt—there was nothing.

She ran to the door that opened to the corridor and took the key out of that, but it was much too big to lock the communicating door. She hunted in the bathroom, but there was evidently no key for that either. She realised she was trembling and sat down on the bed, trying to think. Should she pull the bell-rope and get Yvette to come and ask if she could supply a key? Yvette would now be helping Miss Grantchester to prepare for bed, so Rose was reluctant to disturb her—besides, how could she ask without it seeming like an accusation? It would be tantamount to saying that she didn't trust Philippe, and as she was a guest in the house such an implication would be unforgivable.

For the same reason she could hardly go downstairs again and ask him about it. If she called one of the other servants they would be almost certain to refer the problem to him—probably the key had been lost years ago; after all, there would have been no need to lock it when the adjoining rooms were occupied by husband and wife. It was unlikely that Miss Grantchester, being blind, had any idea that the key was missing. No doubt this room was often used for guests, so it would be even more embarrassing for Rose to be the first one to complain of being unable to lock the door. The more she thought about it the more impossible it seemed to make a fuss about it—besides, had not Philippe himself said that she had nothing to fear from him? He was, she felt certain an honourable man; nevertheless she took a chair and propped it up against the door handle before she undressed and climbed into the huge canopied comfortable bed.

Still she remained alert for some long time, listening for sounds that would indicate that Philippe had entered his room. The Château was old and its timbers seemed to make noises all of their own; a window rattled a little and at quarter-hour intervals a clock chimed downstairs. Once she heard footsteps—there seemed to be a loose floorboard that creaked beneath the carpet just outside her room, but they went away again and Rose decided they were not those of a man anyway, probably Yvette going to her own room.

A shaft of moonlight fell on the angled chair, the door of the adjoining room, it lit the ceramic handle with its pretty design of lilies. She tried to concentrate on it, and once sat up in bed hugging

146

her knees against her chest in alarm as she felt sure she had seen it turn—a slight movement, but was someone there? Was Philippe—? The moon disappeared behind a cloud, leaving the door in darkness. She gave a little sigh; probably it had been no more than a trick of the moonlight that had startled her. She strained her ears for a sound of movement, but a heavy silence had at last settled over the old Château. She lay back on the pillow; she had been tired before she came to bed, and as suddenly as a child she fell asleep.

CHAPTER SIX

Rose awoke to the sound of someone knocking. She lay as if petrified, all her fears of the previous night flooding back as vividly as they had lain in her mind before she fell asleep. Cautiously she opened her eyes, turned her head while still holding the sheets tight up to her chin, uncertain where the sound had come from.

'*Mademoiselle*, are you awake?'

It was a cheery feminine voice that called

to her in French.

'Coming!'

Rose got quickly out of bed, slipped a negligee over her nightie and unlocked the door. A small young maid stood holding an enormous silver tray.

'Good morning, *mademoiselle*. I'm Murielle. Mademoiselle Celia asked me to look after you personally, so I've brought you some breakfast. If you will just get back into bed, please.'

Rose was astonished at the unexpected luxury and obeyed immediately. The girl carried in the tray pressed some attachment beneath it and short supports dropped so that it fitted at exactly the right height over Rose's legs. Her mouth watered as she looked at the croissants, golden butter, toast, marmalade and jam. There was orange juice and a pot of coffee which Murielle now picked up.

'May I pour you coffee, *mademoiselle*? Or would you prefer that I bring you tea or chocolate?'

'Coffee's fine, thank you. Oh, this is lovely!'

Murielle looked pleased. 'I'll come back presently and run your bath for you, *mademoiselle*,' she smiled as she withdrew

148

from the room.

Rose was about to protest that she was quite capable of running her own bath, but Murielle had gone before she had quite recovered from her astonishment at the suggestion. She settled down to enjoy her breakfast, remembering with mounting excitement that this was the wedding day of Kerry and Jacques. Murielle returned about fifteen minutes later and busied herself in the bathroom so that when Rose went in the water was of just the right temperature, scented lightly with *eau de cologne*, a fresh fluffy mat had been spread over the floor and bath towels hung ready to use.

The sheer luxury was a delight, but Rose dared not linger too long. Wrapped in a bath sheet, she went back to the bedroom where Murielle was getting out her bridesmaid's dress; underwear was already lying ready together with her shoes and tights. When Rose was partly dressed Murielle picked up the hairbrush and indicated that she should sit at the dressing-table. The little maid brushed and brushed and under her deft hands the blonde hair shone as if it was lit with gold, and Rose felt cosseted and

149

relaxed and scarcely able to believe it was all happening to her. She complimented Murielle on her skill.

'You have beautiful hair, *mademoiselle*,' Murielle said. 'It is easy to do. Once I thought of training to be a hairdresser, but it meant travelling to Les Virages every day and unfortunately I am not a good traveller—I get sick in cars. So I took the job here instead.'

'Do you like being here?'

'But of course. The Château is a lovely place to work in and Mademoiselle Celia and Monsieur Philippe are most kind—really I am better off here than I would be as a hairdresser because I have no expenses and I get most of my meals included too, as well as uniform.'

Rose glanced at the pretty carriage clock that stood on the dressing-table.

'*Mon Dieu!* Is that the right time?'

Hurriedly she finished dressing and stood in front of the full-length mirror to make sure that she was as neat as a new pin, and in fact was rather pleased with the effect of the dainty apple green gown which suited her lightly tanned complexion perfectly.

'*Très chic!* You look very pretty, *mademoiselle*,' Murielle complimented her.

Rose hurried downstairs to the courtyard where she got into her Mini and drove the short distance to Ste Thérèse. Kerry was almost ready and looking radiant and quite beautiful in her wedding gown. Mrs Langham was fluttering around, convinced that there must be something more that had to be done, though actually there was not. The children, dressed for the occasion as pageboy and tiny bridesmaid, were hopping about restlessly, demanding attention, and had to be constantly watched so that they did not get dirty.

The first part of the ceremony was the signing of the civil contract, and for that they had to go to La Mairie in Les Virages. Shortly after Rose arrived Monsieur and Madame Vieilland drove up, they were to lead the way to the Town Hall. Jacques and his best man had already gone ahead. In the French manner there was no formality about cars; Mr Langham drove his own with his wife beside him and Rose and Kerry sat in the back. Kerry's brother took his own family and Charles stayed behind.

'See you in church,' he grinned as they left.

When they arrived another wedding was

already in progress. They parked in the square outside the ancient stone building, alongside a familiar very dark blue sports car. Rose was surprised; she had not expected that Philippe would be attending this part of the ceremony. He got out, Jacques with him, and together they moved towards Mr Langham's car.

'Where's the best man?' Rose whispered to Kerry.

'Didn't you know? He was practising a parachute jump a day or two ago and managed to break his leg. Philippe is acting in his place,' Kerry grinned mischievously. 'My in-laws are delighted—I almost think they bribed the instructor to make it happen!'

They might be pleased with the turn of events, but Rose was quite disconcerted at the realisation that she would be thrown so closely into Philippe's company. The couple who had just been married emerged through the wide double doors of the Town Hall and stood posing on the steps for photographs to be taken. With them came the Mayor, looking resplendent in his dark suit and a tricolour sash across his portly chest. With affable but solemn dignity he bade farewell to that couple and advanced to greet the new party.

That part of the ceremony was quickly conducted, it was simply a formal legal contract that made Kerry and Jacques man and wife—but from the family's point of view the more important part of the proceedings was still to come. From the Town Hall they drove straight back to the village church, and then began the reverent religious ceremony, with a choir in remarkably good voice and small dark-haired altar boys attendant on the priest. As the wedding service proceeded and Kerry was given away by her father, rings were exchanged, and as they stepped forward together Philippe fell back into place beside Rose. She was intensely aware of him but kept her eyes to the front where Kerry and Jacques knelt before the priest.

The church was packed, it seemed to Rose that almost all the village must be there, and those that had not been inside were waiting to see them come out when the elaborate ceremony was at last completed. There was no doubt that Jacques was a popular young man and his family respected locally—there were smiling expressions of admiration for Kerry, who made a lovely bride. Her naturally good features shone with happiness as she looked at Jacques and read the pride and love that lit his face. Cameras clicked and confetti was thrown, all the time-honoured ritual was carried out.

A large part of the crowd followed them up to the courtyard of the Château where trestle tables had been set out for a buffet lunch; it was to be open house for everyone from the village. There were special chairs set out for the bride and groom and the principal guests, the rest just milled around and helped themselves, but the atmosphere was one of great spontaneous joy and friendliness. Rose noticed Miss Grantchester sitting a little to one side and moved across to her.

'Can I fetch you something to eat, Miss Grantchester?'

'Philippe is doing that, but you can sit and tell me all that's going on. I get the feeling that it's been a really lovely wedding.'

'Oh, it has!' Rose agreed. 'Kerry looked absolutely beautiful—and they're obviously so very much in love.'

'Ah, love! That was a privilege that was granted to me for such a short time. You know, I was engaged to a young man, but he was killed in the war. It was such a terrible waste—all those fine, strong handsome young men wiped out. Just wiped out!'

'It must have been awful for you,' Rose murmured.

'That was the end of love for me, and it was the same for my sister too. She married, of course, and it was a successful partnership, perhaps it was all the better for being entered into in that way.'

'I can't really believe that,' Rose demurred. 'I still think one should marry for love.'

'At least neither my sister nor her husband expected more from their union than it was likely to yield. They entered into it with their eyes open.' Miss Grantchester paused. 'It worries me that Philippe hasn't yet married. I keep telling him—'

She broke off as she heard footsteps approaching, obviously she recognised them as Philippe's. He walked towards them.

'And what is it you keep telling me, Aunt Celia?'

He placed a glass of wine carefully into her hand, making sure her fingers had closed firmly around the stem before withdrawing his hand. Miss Grantchester took a sip before she answered him.

'That it's high time you married, Philippe. You should find some really nice young girl—like Rose here.'

'Alas, I am too late there already.' Philippe's eyes danced mockingly. 'Rose already has a boy-friend. He's here today.'

'You never told me, Rose,' Miss Grantchester said reproachfully.

Rose gave a light laugh to cover her embarrassment to the strange turn the conversation had taken.

'Charles is just an old school friend. He turned up here yesterday. I didn't even know he was coming.'

'Humph!' Miss Grantchester gave a snort. 'That doesn't sound like real opposition to you, Philippe. Woman was made to be conquered. I don't have any time for this new-fangled Women's Lib stuff—you don't believe in that nonsense, do you, Rose?'

'Yes, in some instances I do.'

'That's only because you're so young. Soon change your ideas once you're married.'

'But you were advocating marriage as a partnership, a simple straightforward legal arrangement with no emotional involvement, so surely you don't think of it as a role of subservience?' Rose countered.

'Not subservience, each playing their part in the duet, like a soprano and a tenor singing in harmony, controlled, complementing each other. I would much prefer to see Philippe choose his marriage partner with care and precision than I would risk him bringing home some girl with whom he's become infatuated. After all, his wife would have to be suitable for her position here at the Château.'

'My life is quite different,' said Rose. 'I shall marry only when I fall in love.'

'You're wrong, Rose,' Miss Grantchester persisted. 'You can have a good and contented marriage without all that romantic stuff.'

'I'm sure Philippe agrees with you absolutely,' retorted Rose, a shade tartly.

'Aunt Celia has been advocating marriage for me over the last ten years,' Philippe replied easily. 'It has been one of the few matters on which we have not been in agreement—but you will be relieved to know I have now begun to give the matter some thought.'

'And not before time. I can't understand the way you've been hesitating—'

'My reasons are something I am not prepared to discuss,' Philippe said forcefully. 'Especially here and now.'

It was the first time Rose had ever noticed the slightest rift between Philippe and his great-aunt, and even then they made it appear the merest ripple of a division.

'All right.' Miss Grantchester patted his hand affectionately. 'But don't leave it too long. I should so much like to hold your child in my arms before I die. I'd be happy if I could be sure the line would continue.'

'This is no time to talk of dying,' Philippe reproved her.

He moved away to circulate among the guests. The wedding celebrations went on for a long time, although the bride and her family were English much of what they did that day was in the French tradition. The party continued all the afternoon, the men settled down to a game of *boules*, the children found badminton racquets and skipping ropes or ran about playing boisterous games of hide and seek, chasing each other around the garden, but there was plenty of space for all these activities. The young men even managed to set up an impromptu net for a game of volleyball and Jacques joined in as enthusiastically as all the rest.

As evening approached most of the casual guests departed, leaving only those who were close relatives of the couple and they gathered together for a long meal of many courses, punctuated by various wines. This was held in the ballroom of the Château where a group of local musicians, friends of the Vieillands had set up their instruments in a corner. It was a typical French accordion band and the tunes they favoured were the popular oldies, though they had a few modern songs in their repertoire. Jacques and Kerry were encouraged to lead the dancing, they made their way around the floor to applause and amid teasing laughter, then Philippe came to stand by Rose. He bowed and though his face was serious there was a disquieting twinkle in his eyes as he took her hand and pulled her gently towards him.

'Come, Rose, now it is the turn of the best man and the bridesmaid.'

His arm closed tight around her waist and she could feel the muscles of his chest and arms as he stood poised, listening to the beat of the music, then she was swirled into step with him. He danced with long sweeping steps that carried her around the floor as if she had been as light as thistledown. Several other couples began to join the dancers on the small floor and the band changed to a slower rhythm. It was a smooch. Rose felt Philippe's arms gather her more closely to his chest, subtly holding her so that their two bodies were swaying together in a unison that was exquisitely intimate. He lowered his head so that his cheek brushed hers, and she felt the warmth of his breath as it touched her skin, as sweet as a summer breeze.

For only a moment did she permit herself the luxury of allowing him to hold her so, then as his touch began to have that disconcerting effect that sent her pulses racing in a way that was quite alarming, she jerked her head back and wriggled a little away from his clasp. For her own peace of mind she just dared not allow him to dance with her in such an intimate fashion. It was all very well for him, the contact evoked no deep emotional involvement in him, but it was impossible for her to try to pretend that his touch meant nothing to her.

He looked surprised as she jerked away from him. She saw his eyes harden and a flicker of annoyance crossed his handsome face. For a moment she thought he would leave her there and then, but his manners were too polished for that. He was annoyed, that was evident, but his anger was well controlled; he continued to dance with her, but now held her with the lightest, most remote of holds. The movement that had been like a caress was now a cold rhythmical exercise. Apart from that he made no comment—and there was nothing Rose could say.

'I—I'm sorry,' she began to murmur.

'Please do not apologise,' he said coldly. 'It is I who should apologise. I was simply enjoying the dance, I had no idea you would find it so distasteful. Allow me to escort you back to the safety of your English boy-friend.' He escorted Rose to where Charles was sitting, then with little more than a curt nod, said, 'I shall leave now.'

Discomfited, Rose watched as Philippe moved politely from group to group, saying goodnight, offering good wishes. He kissed Kerry's hand, then crossed the room to bid his usual affectionate goodnight to Miss Grantchester.

'Leaving so early, Philippe?' she heard the old lady remonstrate. 'You're not going into Les Virages again, surely?'

Rose did not catch the whole of his reply, but his final sentence was quite clear.

'You remember that I have to go to London first thing in the morning? I'll be away for about a week. Goodnight, Aunt Celia.'

Miss Grantchester left soon after he did, as if his sudden departure had upset her. Rose felt guiltily that she had been partly responsible for driving him away—but no doubt the lovely brunette in Les Virages would be more responsive to his embrace. The trouble was that deep in her heart Rose knew that she had really been thrilled to be held so close to him. It was certainly not repugnance that had made her push him away from her, but the certain knowledge that such contact could trigger off reactions within her that could so easily get out of control.

'Like to dance?' asked Charles.

She nodded. Anything would be better than sitting here feeling miserable, even lumbering around the floor in that travesty of movement that Charles called dancing. For Rose the evening was flat after Philippe left.

Kerry and Jacques departed for an undeclared destination for their honeymoon. Mr and Mrs Langham and their son and his family had all made arrangements to stay on and spend a week or so at the villa as part of their holiday. They seemed to have no objection to Charles staying with them. With Philippe away Miss Grantchester came to rely more and more on Rose for companionship and usually pressed her to dine with her and spend the evening at the Château in addition to the clerical work she did every morning. Rose found this arrangement quite pleasing, but Charles grumbled about seeing so little of her.

'You're spending far too much time with that old lady, Rose,' he complained. 'I don't mind your being up at the Château for the morning, I know you've taken that on as a job, but you've no need to be there in the afternoon and evening as well.'

'I don't mind.'

'But I do. Anyone would think you

were avoiding me. I'm here on my own all day long.'

'You don't have to stay, Charles,' she pointed out, making her voice gentle to counteract the harshness of the words.

He looked at her sharply. 'Just what do you mean by that?'

'Only what I say. I wouldn't want you to feel in any way—that you should stay on here because—well, because of me.'

'You mean you want to be rid of me?'

'I didn't say that. You're twisting my words. Charles, look at it this way, we've always been good friends. I'd like it to stay that way.'

'As I remember it there was rather more than friendship between us, Rose.'

It was about a week after the wedding and they had been swimming in the river and now lay side by side on the beach. Charles rolled over and put an arm around her, trying to kiss her, but she turned her head to one side.

'No,' she protested.

'Why not? You used to like being kissed, you can't have forgotten, Rose?'

'That's not the point—'

'Aw, come on, darling—just a little kiss, for old times' sake?'

'No. Charles, I must be straight with you. Whatever there was between us is finished.'

'Not for me it isn't. I still love you, Rose. I haven't changed.'

'We were too young—it never really meant anything, you know that. Besides, I wasn't the only girl you kissed at school. There was Marilyn Taylor—'

'You've no need to be jealous of Marilyn—'

'I'm not jealous,' Rose protested. 'It's just that all that—school and the end-of-term dance—it all seems so long ago. It was a different world.' She sighed. 'I suppose I've changed.'

'You certainly have!'

He looked downcast and she felt rather sorry for him, but she knew in her heart that it was his pride that was hurt rather than any deep emotion. Charles, she admitted now, had considered himself a bit of a ladykiller when they were in the sixth form. In that crestfallen mood he looked just an overgrown and disappointed boy.

'Cheer up,' she smiled.

He lay back and looked up at the cloudless blue sky. There was silence between them for a few minutes.

'Rose, how long do you propose to stay here?'

'I don't know. I haven't really thought about it.'

'If you're going back soon, you could give me a lift. I could share the driving and the cost of the petrol. After all, Kerry's married now.'

'Yes. I suppose there's no real need for me to stay on, but it's pleasant here. I like working for Miss Grantchester.'

'Yeah! And living it up at the Château,' he remarked.

Rose laughed. 'That is a luxury to which I'm still not really accustomed. Murielle spoils me atrociously—I don't know how I'll ever settle for looking after myself again.'

'You'll have to, one of these days, though. You mustn't forget that you don't belong there. I'm serious, Rose and believe me, I am only thinking of you.'

'I know what you mean, Charles. It—it's so sort of idyllic up there—I sometimes have to pinch myself to make sure it's not just a dream.'

'I wouldn't like to think you got too much into the clutches of that old woman.'

'You don't understand. It's not like that

at all,' Rose protested.

'It's the first time in your life you've come into close contact with people who are rich and powerful, isn't it?'

'Yes, but—'

'Then just stop and think what's happening to you, Rose. You're already giving more and more of your time to them, more and more of yourself. People like that are used to taking whatever they want.'

'Miss Grantchester's not like that at all. I spend more time with her because—well, because I like her company, as well as knowing that she needs me.'

'Because it's easy too, it's a soft option up there. It's remote from real life.'

'It seems real enough to me Charles. I—I know it can't last for ever, but it's pleasant, even being on the fringe of a world that's so different from anything I've known before.'

'That's what worries me, Rose. You could come to like it too much, so that you wouldn't want to leave. I mean, have you thought any more about going to university? With your "A" levels you could easily get a place.'

She had achieved better results in the examinations than she had expected.

'I wouldn't want to go this year, anyway. I want to be right away from studying and all that for a time, try to sort myself out. It's different for you, you know exactly what you're going to do.'

Charles would be going to Oxford soon and planned to go into his father's business when he had his degree.

'Yeah. Well, I don't need to be back for a few weeks yet, so I'll stay on a little longer—just in case you change your mind.'

'What about?'

'Anything,' he replied enigmatically. 'I still have a feeling you may yet be glad to have me around. I wonder if I can get some work around here—grape picking or something?'

'I've no idea. Come on, let's have another swim.'

Rose was glad they had had that conversation, that the air had been cleared between them, though some of the points he had made lingered in her mind. He was quite right to remind her not to be beguiled by life at the Château, though she did not feel it to be as remote from reality as he had suggested. It was her feeling for Philippe that was unreal, that was what she had to be wary of; it was Philippe, not Miss Grantchester, who could so easily ensnare her. She felt she was being very practical as she acknowledged to herself exactly where the danger lay, acknowledged that she could easily fall in love with him and that could lead to nothing but heartbreak. Both his attitude to marriage and that of Miss Grantchester's reinforced the certainty that to love him would be fatal for her, but now that the problem had been honestly identified she had every confidence she could keep her head and look on it objectively.

The new understanding between herself and Charles was a relief. If he wished to stay on, knowing there would never be more than a brotherly and sisterly affection between them, that was fine, and to cement their new relationship Rose made arrangements for them to do some sightseeing together the following afternoon.

They visited a medieval fortified town, close packed within a well-preserved high stone wall, protected from old enemies perhaps but certainly not from tourists. Its narrow streets with overhanging upper stories to the houses were thronged with people, who overflowed from cafés or lounged outside at small tables, sipping wines and *apéritifs*. The souvenir shops held the usual miscellany of pottery on which was written the name of this *ville pittoresque*. Rose bought a few postcards and they sat at one of the pavement restaurants sipping cool drinks—beer for Charles and lemon for Rose, and since she was sending the cards to mutual friends they thought up amusing comments together which made them laugh a great deal.

They looked into a very old church which squatted benevolent as a mother hen in the middle of a small square, shading the old people who sat on its steps whiling away the late afternoon with gossip. At every corner of the solid grey edifice were pots and hanging baskets spilling out colour with cascades of begonias, petunias, bougainvilleas and geraniums, a wealth of reds, purples, whites, pink and orange, bright as the stained glass of its windows.

It was not an afternoon to be hurried. The heat and the crowds were both restrictive and Rose and Charles wandered, at peace with one another and with their surroundings, drinking in the sights and sounds, the smells and the tastes that would always remind them of France. It was therefore quite late when they finally drove back to the Château. Charles was at the wheel of the little green Mini.

'Drop me off at the Château and you can take the Mini back to the villa,' said Rose.

'Okay. That was a great afternoon, Rose.'

'I enjoyed it too.'

They drove up to the courtyard and evidently Philippe had just returned too. His very dark blue sports car stood in the drive and he was taking out his suitcase. He looked towards them as Charles braked the Mini. Philippe gave a curt nod in their direction and picked up his case, ready to walk into the house. Rose thought he looked tired and tense, perhaps business had not gone smoothly—and then, of course, he had had a long journey.

'I wonder if I might have a word with you?' Charles said to Philippe, to Rose's great surprise.

Philippe stopped and lifted one quizzical eyebrow, attentive but not too friendly.

'I wondered if there might be any work for me at the grape harvest,' Charles asked.

'It's something I've always wanted to do and as I'm here and free—'

'Sorry,' came the reply. 'You're too late.'

'Too late? Surely you haven't even started picking yet?'

'We haven't. But the days of harvesting by hand have gone. We pick most of our crop by machine nowadays—not so romantic, I agree, but much more efficient and cheaper. All the other extra labour we need we recruit from within the village, no outsiders at all now.'

'Oh.' Charles looked crestfallen.

'If it's work you're looking for, you won't find much in this area—wasting your time. There might be some needed in the vineyards in the more hilly areas. It's not too far, twenty or thirty miles—you might be lucky there.'

'Thanks. I'll think about it.'

Philippe turned towards Rose.

'Are you dining with us tonight, Rose?'

'Yes, but we didn't know you'd be back—'

'That makes no difference. I'll probably have to go out again later this evening, so Aunt Celia will be glad of your company. Come.'

His gesture ushered her into the Château. She turned back to smile a farewell at Charles and saw by the look on his face that he felt that much of what he had warned her of was being proved to be true. She almost felt herself that she was being manipulated—yet how pleasant it was to enter her room and find Murielle there with the bath water all ready for her to step into, with the dress she had worn the previous day washed and ironed and returned to its hanger with as much care as if it had been a model instead of one of her own making. Her clean undies were lying on the bed—the sheer luxury of it all was something to be savoured—and if it was to be but a brief encounter, then all the more reason to enjoy it while she could, Rose decided.

She undressed and stepped into the bath, allowing herself the sensual pleasure of wallowing in the scented water. A sound came from the adjoining wall. It was Philippe singing in his bath, a vibrant reminder that he was back and occupying those rooms that were adjacent to hers—too close for her peace of mind. She would remember to place the chair against the door handle tonight.

173

CHAPTER SEVEN

Rose regarded her limited wardrobe with a lack of enthusiasm, she had brought few dresses with her, not that she had many in any case. Certainly she had never given any thought, when packing to come to Chandelle and stay with Kerry, that she might find herself dining night after night in the style she did here at the Château. The only thing that could be said in favour of those she had brought was that they were all fresh and summery looking. That evening she selected a cotton dress of cornflower blue, sprigged with tiny bunches of white and pale blue; it had a fitting bodice with a neat collar and tiny capped sleeves and the flowing skirt was particularly becoming. She had bought it in the Christmas sale so at least it seemed to her to have an elegance that surpassed her home-made efforts. Murielle appeared as if by magic to brush her hair and Rose chatted with her, telling her where she had been that day. Murielle knew the town well, she had relatives living there.

'You should go there on the Jour de Fête in May,' she told Rose. 'It's a great carnival. There's a procession led by Le Suisse—he wears a cocked hat and carries a staff and looks very grand, and there are bands. Last year there was a troupe of Arlésiennes on horseback—they were fabulous!'

Murielle was a bright companion and Rose always enjoyed talking to her— besides, it was a good exercise for her French. When she was with Miss Grantchester they always talked in English. As soon as she was ready she went downstairs. Miss Grantchester as usual was in the drawing room, with Gigi at her feet and the table with her customary *apéritif* had already been conveniently placed at her side.

'Is that you, Rose? Have you had a pleasant afternoon?'

Rose told the old lady where she had been and took pains to make her descriptions as lively and vivid as possible. They sat on talking for some time.

'Philippe is back—did you know?' said Miss Grantchester. 'He's late, but I expect he's looking through his correspondence. I don't know why he can't leave that until after dinner.'

Rose remembered that Philippe had said he might go out later, but she avoided making such a suggestion.

'He knows I like to have my meals on time—besides, it's so difficult for the chef. Ah, I think I hear him coming.'

Rose too had heard the quick footsteps in the hall. The door was swung open and Philippe walked in. At once it seemed as if the room sprang to life, it was not simply that he was a big man, tall and athletic, it was something in the vitality of his personality that seemed to radiate around him. The tenseness she had read in his face that afternoon seemed to have been washed away, discarded with his smart business suit, and he now looked fresh and relaxed though still immaculate in a freshly laundered short-sleeved shirt and lightweight trousers of lovat green.

'Sorry I'm late, Aunt Celia,' he apologised with the air of one who knows he will be forgiven. He bent and kissed her dryly powdered cheek and taking her hands in his gave them a loving squeeze. He drew his aunt to her feet.

'Shall we go in to dinner straight away?

I had my *apéritif* while I looked through my mail.'

He escorted Miss Grantchester through to the dining room and helped her into her usual place at the table. Rose followed and took her seat opposite, sitting on Philippe's left hand. At once the servant brought in the hors-d'oeuvre. As always the food was excellent. During the early part of the meal Miss Grantchester questioned him about some aspects of the London side of the business and he answered in detail, keeping her up to date on a variety of changes and improvements that were being introduced. She seemed to know exactly what he was talking about, though to Rose, who had no business background, it was almost incomprehensible. They talked too of other members of the board of directors and senior members of staff, one or two of whom had retired and whom Miss Grantchester seemed to know personally. She was delighted to hear details of the presentations and farewell parties that had been given in honour of their long and valued service. It was as they reached the sweet course that Philippe brought the conversation back to Chandelle.

'And how has everything been here at

the Château in my absence?'

'We've managed admirably without you, my boy. In fact I can honestly say I've missed you much less than usual—but that's been because I've had the company of Rose.'

Philippe turned and inclined his head towards her, raising his glass. 'Then I must drink a toast to that young lady. Thank you, Rose.'

Rose felt the colour rising in her cheeks. She hated the way she blushed when compliments were paid to her.

'I tell you, Rose is an absolute treasure, Philippe. She's made a world of difference in my life.'

'Oh, Miss Grantchester,' protested Rose, 'I've done very little really.'

'Nonsense, you've done a lot, and what's more, you always do things so charmingly, you don't make me feel I'm an old nuisance—'

'I should think not!' Rose exclaimed. 'Because you're always so nice to me. I've enjoyed being here—it's been a wonderful experience.'

Philippe looked at her sharply, catching something in the tone of her voice as well as in her words.

'An experience that we hope will be continued for a long, long time,' he said.

'Well, that's what I was about to mention,' Rose murmured, mindful of her recent conversation with Charles. 'Obviously I can't stay on here indefinitely.'

'Don't dare talk of leaving,' Miss Grantchester exclaimed. 'You're not going to desert me, surely?'

'No, not immediately. But—well, I have to think about starting my career.'

'What career is that?' Philippe asked.

'I—I'm not really sure yet. But you know, I'm nearly nineteen—'

'Ah, so old!' His voice was mocking.

'I know I can't expect you to stay indefinitely, Rose,' Miss Grantchester said. 'But I didn't raise this subject to speak about you leaving. You've always said you don't know what you're going to do, all I ask is that you stay on with me until you have made up your mind. That's not unreasonable, is it?'

Rose shook her head, forgetting for the moment that Miss Grantchester could not see her.

'Rose has agreed, Aunt Celia,' said Philippe. 'May I say we shall both be very grateful. My aunt's happiness is of

179

great importance to me.' Then with a note of impudence in his voice he added, 'Apart from the fact that it means a quieter life for me too.'

Miss Grantchester rose to his challenge. 'Nonsense, Philippe! Don't think that I shall relax my interest in your affairs in any way. On the contrary, I shall continue to keep as tight a rein on you as possible, until you have the good sense to take on a wife.'

Philippe wiped his mouth with his napkin and threw it on the table beside him. They had all finished eating. He evidently did not intend to enter again into a conversation on that subject, and for that Rose was grateful.

'Perhaps you ladies would like to take coffee in the drawing-room?' he suggested.

'And what about you, Philippe?' asked Miss Grantchester, though the note of disapproval in her voice suggested that she knew the answer to her question even before she asked it, just as Rose did.

'I have to go out for a short time. I shall not join you for coffee,' he replied easily.

Miss Grantchester's lips shut in a firm line. Her disapproval was very evident, though she made no further comment.

Indeed it seemed to Rose that she made a special effort to chat amiably and inconsequentially as they sat on together alone for the rest of the evening. Feeling rather sorry for her, Rose did her best to keep the atmosphere lively, though for some reason that evening it was more difficult than previously. It was as though some part of Philippe's presence had remained hauntingly between them.

The next two days were uneventful, though Rose spent rather more time at the Villa Ste Thérèse than usual. The Langhams had by then left to return to England, but Charles was living there alone. Now it was almost time for Kerry and Jacques to return from their honeymoon and Rose was determined that the house should be clean and bright to welcome them. Charles was by no means the tidiest of young men and in the days he had been there on his own he had happily ignored the accumulation of dust.

Mr Langham had told Kerry and Jacques they could make their home in the villa for as long as they wished. 'I make only one condition—that there shall be a bed for your mother and me when we come on holiday,' he had added with dry humour.

'I guess we might find a corner for you,' Kerry grinned.

Rose had been delighted that the old family unity had been so completely restored. With some help from Charles she had the house bright and shining and on the evening the young couple returned she cooked an appetising supper. As always when she and Kerry met up together they talked and joked and time whisked away in the pleasantest possible way. It passed so quickly that Rose got quite a shock when she noticed how late it was.

'It's high time I got back!' she exclaimed, jumping to her feet.

'You could stay here,' Kerry said. 'There's plenty of room now.'

'That's right—why not move back to the villa?' asked Charles, as if he had a perfect right to invite her.

Rose smiled. 'I may do that in a day or two, haven't any clear plans yet.'

'I'll be glad to have you here for as long as you want to stay,' Kerry offered. 'Though as soon as Jacques goes back to his regiment he's going to see if he can find some accommodation for me so we can be nearer each other.'

'I see,' Rose said thoughtfully. 'In that

case perhaps I should think about going home myself.'

'There's no hurry. I merely mentioned it because if you're going to stay on it might be a bit lonely when Charles goes back to England. Unless you stay on at the Château.'

'I'll have to think about it,' said Rose. 'Now I really must get back there. I'm afraid one of the servants may be waiting to lock up.'

'I'll drive up with you,' Charles offered. 'Wouldn't mind a walk back. It's a beautiful evening.'

It took only a few minutes in her little Mini and when they arrived at the Château Charles locked up the car and handed her the keys.

'Thanks. Goodnight, Charles.'

'Wait one minute,' said Charles.

Before she could move a step his arms had closed around her and he was kissing her. With some annoyance she turned her face from him. She didn't want to start an undignified struggle there in the moonlight in the old courtyard. Charles knew how she felt about him—he wasn't playing fair.

'No, Charles. We agreed, didn't we? No emotional involvement.'

'Okay, okay,' he laughed lightly. 'I didn't mean anything—just wanted to kiss you, what's so wrong in that? You're getting very prudish.'

'Maybe,' she seized on the stigma readily. 'Call it that if you want.'

'If you didn't look so pretty I wouldn't want to kiss you,' Charles pointed out.

'That's right, put the blame on me—but I'm not going to quarrel with you. I really do mean it, though. I want no involvement with you.'

'Is there someone else, then?'

'No.'

If it was a lie it was not deliberate. She purposefully avoided looking squarely at the turbulence of her feelings for Philippe. It was as if her emotions had been stretched out and tied in knots and she felt helpless to unravel them. Only of one thing was she certain—she had no wish to spend the rest of her life with Charles. Though she liked him, there was no way in which she found him exciting—there was no thrill when he kissed her—she would rather remain single, become a career woman, than be tied to him.

'No, there's no one else. I'm just trying to find my own identity—you did the same when you set off to travel across Europe this summer.'

'But I was eager to come back to you, Rose.'

'That's only temporary, you know that, Charles. When you get to Oxford, with all those girls around, you'll be glad when we're not bound to one another in any way. Now I really must go in.'

'Okay. Just one light peck on your cheek, then.'

That made her laugh. It allowed Charles to feel unbeaten and she did like him, though there was no love in it. She leaned towards him and received his brotherly kiss.

'Goodnight, Rose. See you tomorrow.'

With a wave of her hand she ran up the steps and in through the door. Quietly she tiptoed across the silent hall up the wide staircase and along the corridor to her room. She passed the door of Philippe's room and wondered if he was back yet, but there was no sound. She opened the door gently, and it opened inwards. She was about to reach out for the light switch when she realised there was someone already in the room. The figure of a man rose from a chair by the window, clearly silhouetted in the bright moonlight. A shocked gasp choked in Rose's throat, and she almost screamed.

'It's all right, Rose.' It was Philippe. His voice was quiet and reassuring. 'I just wanted to have a word with you.'

He moved to the bedside and switched on a pink-shaded lamp which gave a pleasantly subdued illumination to the room.

'What do you want?' she asked.

'I'll come to that presently.'

'Is something the matter with Miss Grantchester?'

As the thought occurred to her she moved further into the room and the door closed behind her. She took only a few steps towards where Philippe stood, close to the window, so that she could see his face more clearly. His expression was serious, the deep dark eyes stared back at her and that small scar shone like a tiny white mark on the bridge of his arrogant nose, against the deeply tanned skin. She could read nothing from his expression.

'No.'

Momentarily she was relieved, but as he paused again Rose felt her uneasiness growing. Surely it must be something serious that had caused him to sit here in her room, waiting for her? Unexpectedly she sensed a loneliness in him and an anger.

'Is—is it something I've done, Philippe?' she asked.

He gave a short harsh laugh, a sound that unnerved her, yet she could not think what it could be. What did he mean? He turned from her to stare out of the window and she moved closer, wondering what he was looking at. Down below the courtyard was bathed in moonlight, she could see her car parked at one side. Suddenly she realised that Philippe must have been watching her as she and Charles had said goodnight. But why should that concern him?

'Your young man was very affectionate tonight,' said Philippe.

'Charles is affectionate by nature,' she answered lightly.

She was not prepared to discuss her relationship with Charles tonight. It was not any concern of Philippe's, but his reaction took her completely by surprise. He moved swiftly, his arms closed around her and pulled her close, pinioning her tightly against his chest. She gasped, and in that same moment when her mouth was slightly open his lips pressed down on hers with a kiss of such passionate intensity that it took her breath away.

One of his hands slipped down to rest on the lower part of her back and her whole body seemed to be held suspended against the hardness of his masculine frame. Her suppleness, in that moment when she was held there, was relaxed so that she felt as if moulded against him, fitting to him so closely as to seem almost a part of him.

Her heartbeat quickened till it felt like thunder in her breast, instinctively she responded to the passion that had leapt in him, his desire communicated itself powerfully with the gentle movement of his lips against her mouth. The intensity of feeling was like nothing she had ever experienced before, she began to tremble, terror rose sharply in her heart, in her brain. She sensed the danger in this situation, knew that it could all too easily swamp all her preconceived ideas. Primitive emotions in her were making a mockery of those moral values she had been so ready to assume to be right.

Every fibre of her being longed for this exquisite embrace to go on and on for ever. Her pulses raced with an emotion that more than matched that of the man who caressed her with such delicious skill. She longed to give herself utterly to him, yet her conscience began to impinge upon her, her mind refused to accept the joy that was racing through her body. It demanded that she must resist.

She jerked back her head, struggled to free herself and pushed with all her might against his chest. Immediately his grip loosened. Though his arms still encircled her, they now seemed to be supporting her, and she became aware that she was trembling.

'You had no right to do that,' she whispered hoarsely.

'Charles kissed you goodnight,' he pointed out with a touch of mockery.

'Not like that!'

He gave a light laugh.

'I'm glad to hear it. I got the impression you did not actually—dislike my kiss.'

'You took me by surprise.'

'Ah!' There was a wealth of meaning in that ejaculation. 'You like to be kissed only when you are expecting it? But if I had said, Rose, may I kiss you?—what would you have replied?'

'No,' she said shortly.

'Exactly,' he said. 'And that would have deprived both of us of a very enlightening as well as a pleasant experience.'

Despite her rejection she realised that he had noted with evident satisfaction her immediate pleasure in his caresses. She was so shaken and unsure of herself that she began to feel angry.

'And did you sit here waiting for me—in my bedroom—' she managed to put an emphatic scorn into her words for which she was quite pleased, 'just to see if you could kiss me?'

'I hoped that would happen,' he replied. 'But before you jump to conclusions let me assure you that my intentions were, as they say, strictly honourable.'

'It's a pity your behaviour didn't match up to your words, then,' she snapped.

His hands fell to his sides. He stepped back and cleared his throat then spoke with slow deliberation.

'I waited here, so that we might not be disturbed, because I wish to ask you to marry me.'

She gasped, and stared at him incredulously.

'It has seemed to me that you could

190

fit into the Château quite happily,' he continued. 'My aunt, as you must be aware, is very fond of you. I have often thought that it would be a good thing to marry an English girl, just as my grandfather did. You would have every comfort. If you are agreeable, we could make it very soon.'

Her distress deepened. What nonsense was this he was talking? Philippe seemed to take her answer for granted and moved forward again, holding open his arms to her, but she stepped back quickly. He could not play with her emotions like that. What he was suggesting was obviously just one of those *mariages de convenance* by which he set such great store. That was a subject on which they were poles apart—he didn't even speak the same language as she did when it came to love. There was no doubt he was adept, experienced and skilled at lovemaking—but he had not spoken even one word of affection, let alone expressed any love for her.

'No, Philippe.'

He stood stock still. Rose could see tenseness in his attitude, guessed he had never for one moment imagined she would refuse his proposal. By his standards no

191

doubt the deal was a good one—but it was not like that for her. Without affection, without love, his offer was meaningless and quite unthinkable.

'I realise this has come as a surprise to you, Rose. I should not have approached you so abruptly and no doubt you are tired—'

'I am tired,' she admitted. 'I—I suppose I should thank you for the honour you've paid me, but—'

'Don't say any more just now. I shall give you time to think it over,' he said.

'Thank you, but I'm sure I shan't change my mind.'

He clicked his heels together military fashion, in that rather old-fashioned way that he had, and bowed slightly.

'In that case there is nothing more to be said. Goodnight, Rose.'

His head was held high, his shoulders squared, as if he held himself closely in check. His pride had been struck a great blow, she knew that, and probably her rejection had made him angry too. She was sorry that it should be so, but knew in all honesty that she could not have given him any other answer. He paused at the door with his hand on the handle—for one emotional moment she wished that he would turn back. There was still a part of her that longed for him—if only he could have said some word of love, how different it could have been! With what joy she would have sped across the room, into his arms—she would have agreed whatever his terms. He could have picked her up then and there and carried her over to the great bed—

He opened the door without a backward glance, walked out and closed it softly behind him. She felt bereft, empty, and her heart cried out after him—I love you, I love you, Philippe, I love you. She sat down in the chair and looked out into the moonlit courtyard. She longed for him, yet she had sent him away. If she had accepted she knew that her life would have been an alternation of ecstasy and agony. There would have been the joy of loving him, but also the deep soul-destroying misery that he did not return her love. She imagined those nights when he would be away in Les Virages—for she had no doubts that this loveless marriage, this soulless union, would have required no curtailment of what he thought of as his normal way of life. She sat on for a long,

long time staring out into the emptiness of the night.

Charles had been right. There was an insidiousness in this luxurious way of life, she could so easily be caught under the spell of the Château and of its occupants—indeed, in a way that had already happened, for had she not admitted to herself just now that she had fallen in love with Philippe? The way of life of the du Caine family was very different from that to which she was accustomed, she had almost been beguiled by it, but her integrity had triumphed. Slowly she undressed and got into bed.

Sleep was a long way from her mind, but one thing became more and more certain. She must leave Chandelle. She must go home. Tomorrow if possible she must go. She would know no peace of mind until she was away from here—there was so much that she would regret leaving, but she must get away. She would have to give some reason to Miss Grantchester, of course. She wondered if Philippe had discussed his proposal with his aunt—but that seemed unlikely, remembering how he had abruptly ended any such conversation in the past.

Certainly Rose had no intention of mentioning the fact. She resolved to say that she had received an urgent letter from her mother asking her to return home at once. Indeed it scarcely seemed to be a lie, for surely if her mother had known the circumstances she would have written immediately on just those lines. The thought of home helped to calm her, and eventually she fell asleep.

CHAPTER EIGHT

Charles was delighted when she told him she would be returning home. He looked as if he was about to question her about this sudden decision, but she silenced him.

'Don't ask me why. I just feel it's the right thing to do.'

'Okay. I'll throw my things into my rucksack.'

That was precisely what he did. Rose herself packed with less care than usual. She had not seen Philippe at breakfast, for which she was grateful. He had apparently gone to the office early and she surmised that he would be glad that, since she had refused his proposal, she did not stay on at the Château. It would have been acutely embarrassing for both of them.

Miss Grantchester accepted Rose's excuse that she had received an urgent summons from home, though she said more than once how very sorry she was about it.

'Is there any chance that you may be able to return to us?'

'I'm afraid not—at least not for a long time.'

'You'll always be welcome, my dear. I shall miss you, but I do understand and I hope it is nothing too serious. You will write as soon as you get home, won't you? The roads are so dangerous, I shall worry until I hear from you.'

'I'll go carefully. Charles will be with me so we can share the driving, but I'll write as soon as I can,' Rose promised.

'You've no idea how much I shall miss you. Philippe will too, you know. Have you spoken to him?'

'No. But I'm sure he'll understand,' said Rose. The words held more meaning than Miss Grantchester could guess.

If Kerry was puzzled at the abruptness of Rose's departure she made no comment. She had seen Jacques off on the train that morning to rejoin his unit and was sure before long she would be able to move somewhere close to him. Meanwhile she was busy with the washing she had brought back from their holiday and beginning to plan things she must get ready for the baby. She gave Rose a warm hug.

'It's meant so much to me, having you here. Everything seemed to be such a mess before you arrived and now it's all lovely—I can't thank you enough, Rose.'

'I didn't do much.'

'Don't you believe it. It was your influence with the du Caines that won Jacques' parents round so quickly.'

'Nonsense. It was just that they saw how lucky they were to be getting such a nice daughter-in-law.'

'Dear Rose! Anyway, come back and stay with us any time you like.'

The car journey was quite quick. They didn't stop, but took turns at driving and slept as best they could alternately. By the evening of the following day Rose backed the little green Mini into the driveway of her parents' house. She had dropped

Charles off at his home on the way and she had telephoned her mother as soon as they disembarked from the boat at Dover, so she was expected.

It was the warmest of welcomes. Her parents were both delighted to have her back. There was a delicious casserole of beef, one of her favourite meals, keeping hot in the oven ready for her, to be followed by some of her mother's apple pie, the pastry lighter than anyone else seemed to make it. Rose was glad she was hungry, they would have been so disappointed if she had not been able to eat and enjoy the food so lovingly prepared. On the journey they had stopped for only the briefest of snacks and yesterday she had not felt like eating at all. A deep sadness had settled on her spirit, knowing that every mile the little car travelled it took her farther and farther away from Chandelle, from the Château—and most of all, from Philippe.

At home she relaxed and it was heavenly to be looked after again as her mother fussed around. She answered the multitude of questions. Had she had a good time? How was Kerry? How did the wedding go? She told them a lot about Chandelle and the villa, a little about the Château and Miss Grantchester, briefly mentioned Philippe but said not a word about his proposal. That was something she was determined to try and forget. Mrs Robinson for her part told Rose all about the small local events that had happened in the town while she had been away. There was just a light spicing of scandal, but mostly it was about jam-making and new babies and Dad's bowls competition and what the weather had done to the flowers and vegetables in the garden.

Rose was interested, happy just to sit around and talk and listen for a few days. Then she decided, even before her father began to ask her about it, that she must make some plans for the future. Despite the fact that her 'A' levels were good enough to gain her a place in a university it was now a bit late to apply and anyway she still did not want that. Jobs, however, seemed to be hard to come by, especially as she had no skill at typing or shorthand or any other clerical work. She looked through the local paper every morning. There was one job as a dentist's receptionist, another as a snack-bar attendant, either of which she felt she could cope with, but they both sounded rather dull. She telephoned a firm which was asking for car owners as sales representatives and it was arranged that she should go for an interview at a hotel a few miles away.

When she went to find out more about it she knew almost immediately that she would never be able to do it. It entailed selling a product in which she had no faith whatever—in fact she decided quite early on, despite the enthusiasm of the promoter, that she would find it was almost like committing robbery to ask people to part with hard-earned money to buy it. The man who interviewed her was keen for her to accept, he even suggested that she should dine with him that evening when he said he felt sure he could resolve any doubts she had about it—but the way he made that suggestion only increased her disinclination to take the job.

She drove back home, telling herself it was early days yet, she ought not to feel so dispirited. The misery was that she could not help harping back to the recent happy days in Chandelle, and she imagined Miss Grantchester walking around the beautiful Château in the brilliant sunshine, aided by her golden-haired Gigi. It was late

September now, probably the grape harvest would be in full swing, Philippe might be spending more time around the vineyards than usual—she had been looking forward to being there for that annual event.

Philippe! If only she could get him out of her thoughts! She had to accept that Chandelle was in the past, finished and she must try to forget. So much had happened in the past weeks, she had led such a very different life, and now it was over, but the one great reality was the constant ache in her heart. She tried to console herself that it was better to have loved and lost than never to have loved at all. She was too young to find herself locked in the grip of precious memories, but somehow she felt sure she would never again meet anyone like Philippe du Caine.

She turned the corner of the street that led to her home. There was a car parked outside her house—and it wasn't her father's. She stared at the long low powerful sports car of very, very dark blue and could scarcely believe her eyes. She drew the little green Mini to a halt behind it and slowly got out. Definitely it was Philippe's car—her heart was beating fast as she let herself into the house.

'Is that you, Rose? Come and see who's here in the lounge,' her mother's voice called.

As if mesmerised Rose did as she was bidden. Philippe had just risen to his feet and was standing beside the settee, where he must have been sitting beside Mrs Robinson, drinking tea. He placed his cup on the tray.

'Rose!'

In two strides he was across the room, taking her hand in both of his, and the warm pressure of his fingers made the blood course with tingling excitement through every fibre of her being. She looked up at him, at his handsome face with its healthy tanned skin, the aquiline nose with the small scar, those clear-cut features that had haunted her dreams were a reality once more. And his eyes, dark brown as bitter chocolate, were regarding her with that penetrating expression she had come to know so well, as if he was determined to read her very thoughts. It was impossible to meet the intensity of his gaze. She felt shy beneath their searching inquiry.

'Hello, Philippe.'

'We've been having the most delightful

chat,' her mother's voice chimed into the silence that had fallen between them. 'Isn't this a wonderful surprise, dear?'

'Yes, indeed,' Rose murmured.

Her heart raced as she thought—why? Why has he come here? What can I say to him?

'Come and have a cup of tea.'

Rose was glad of the normality of her mother's suggestion. Philippe at last released her hand and she sat down in one of the big chintz-covered armchairs—which was necessary because her knees felt so wobbly. Her mother lifted the tea-pot, then hesitated.

'I think I should make a fresh pot.' She jumped to her feet and was at the door before Rose could stop her. 'I'm sure you two have so much to talk about. I'll just boil up the kettle—won't be long.'

Mrs Robinson was evidently excited. She went out, closing the door behind her. How much did she know? What had Philippe been saying to her? Rose wondered. She shot him a questioning glance.

'Surprised to see me, Rose?' he asked gently.

She nodded. 'I thought we had said all

that needed to be said. I thought you would understand why I left so suddenly.'

'On the contrary, I feel there is a great deal more that should be said between us, my dear Rose—but I shall not pursue that further at the moment.'

He leaned back on the settee, looking so relaxed and at ease that she felt quite annoyed with him. It seemed unfair that while his very presence awoke in her these racing, highly disturbed emotions, he should be able to approach her so coolly.

'You are looking very beautiful,' he said softly.

The words came with a gratifying depth of feeling, almost as if they emanated from deep in his throat. He was looking at her with eyes half closed, his voice and expression reminded her that the last time they had been together he had taken her so closely into his arms that she had felt the beat of his heart, had known how strongly his desire for her pulsed through his body, as in fact it had through hers. She blushed at the memory.

'You have not forgotten, have you, Rose.'

It was a statement rather than a question.

She knew she would never forget the excitement of that moment, but it had been simply a physical attraction on his part. She knew she was not by any means the first girl to have aroused him, there was a very sensual masculinity in Philippe and that had nothing whatever to do with love. Not a single word of love had he spoken, and that was still what she yearned for. It was a relief when she heard her mother's footsteps approaching along the hallway.

Philippe leapt to open the door for her, Mrs Robinson was more and more impressed. He hovered beside her while she poured the tea and handed a cup to Rose before sitting down again. He took another cup himself and complimented Mrs Robinson on the delicious homemade cakes she offered him.

'Where are you staying?' Rose asked.

'At the Maid's Head.'

It was the only five-star hotel in the area, situated on the outskirts of the city a few miles from the little market town where the Robinsons lived.

'I should be honoured if you would all dine there with me this evening,' he added.

'Oh, there's no need for you to do that,'

Mrs Robinson beamed. 'Why don't you have supper here with us? It would only be simple, homely fare, of course—'

'I'm sure it would be delightful, much better food than I shall be able to offer you at the hotel, nevertheless I could not dream of putting you to so much trouble. No—if I may use your telephone I will book a table for four.'

By the time Mr Robinson arrived home from school—he was headmaster of the Middle School in the town—all arrangements had been made. Mrs Robinson trotted off to the kitchen again to brew up yet another pot of tea for her husband, though this time Philippe's good manners could not stretch to his taking any more. Rose sat back, quietly observant and with considerable astonishment and a strange pleasure, saw her father fall under the spell of charm that Philippe seemed intent on weaving about them all.

Before long he had discovered that Mr Robinson was a keen bowls player and they discussed at some length the respective merits of the French style of *boules* as compared with the English version which required such a special green. From bowls they moved on to music, and there it seemed they had an interest in common. Philippe discoursed knowledgeably on the works of some of Mr Robinson's favourite composers, yet at the same time listened to the older man's views with respect and interest. By the time they were ready to set off to the Maid's Head, Rose was aware that both her parents were very deeply impressed by Philippe—and not a little puzzled as to his relationship with their daughter. There was, luckily, no chance to discuss it with them.

Mr Robinson took his car; Philippe's was really only a two-seater anyway. Inevitably that meant that Rose accompanied Philippe. The familiar leathery smell of the car awakened memories of that first time she had ridden in it. She had decided then that this man was high-handed, used to getting his own way, arrogant, chauvinist, aggressively masculine and nothing that had happened since had made her change her mind, but the extraordinary thing was that, in spite of all, she loved him. She felt silent and shy now. Philippe, however, seemed to be in the best of good humours. If, as she supposed, there was some specific reason for this visit, he made no mention of it, but instead began to talk about Chandelle.

'I saw your friend Kerry, a few days ago,' he told her. 'I gave her a lift to the station to catch her train. She will be with Jacques now, I imagine.'

'That's great! She'll be so happy.' Rose paused and regarded him thoughtfully. 'It was kind of you to take her to the train.'

A slow smile lifted a corner of his mouth. 'I had to visit her to get your address. It was no trouble to me to run her into Les Virages.'

No, Rose thought, remembering how often and for what reason he went there so often, but if he guessed her train of thought, Philippe gave her no time to brood on it.

'Kerry sent you her love. She was telling me of some of the pranks you used to get up to together. She has a lively sense of humour.'

'She has that,' Rose agreed.

She wondered just what her friend had been saying about her, but Philippe did not enlighten her and she would not ask. It began to rain and he switched on the windscreen wipers. She changed the subject by asking what the weather was like in Chandelle. It was an unwise move, for as he began to describe the pleasant days of late summer there, with the start of the grape harvest, the longing to be back was difficult to stifle. Fortunately before long they arrived at the Maid's Head.

The evening must have been considered highly successful from Philippe's point of view, Rose had to acknowledge. He consolidated the high opinion her parents had begun to form about him into a deeper and deeper conviction that he was not only a man of pleasing personality, but also one of wealth and power and moreover a man of culture, well educated and with a breadth of knowledge that more than matched that of her father. Mr Robinson could scarcely help being impressed, while her mother would have eaten out of Philippe's hand if he had asked her to do so.

Rose remained rather quiet during the meal, allowing Philippe and her parents to do most of the talking. Since Philippe sat opposite her at the table it was impossible to avoid looking at him, and as she watched his face, the love she had been trying to smother in her heart sprang more and more vibrantly to life. By this time she was sure that he was going to ask her again to marry him—would she have the strength to resist him when that happened?

Philippe did not broach the subject that evening, but when the time came for Rose and her parents to part he made sure that he and Rose were a few steps behind. That was not difficult; Mr and Mrs Robinson were the souls of tact and obviously they had quickly acknowledged that there was something between their daughter and this handsome young man. Philippe took her hand in his and deliberately drew her aside.

'I will call on you tomorrow afternoon, Rose,' he said. He lifted his hand to silence her when she would have spoken. 'In fairness to me, you must allow me one more opportunity to ask you that same question. I promise that whatever your answer is then, I will accept it. If you are sure that your response must still be the same I will not press you, I will leave at once.'

'I—I don't know what to say.'

He was still holding her hand.

'Of course you don't, Rose. My turning up today was so unexpected, but I had to do it this way—if I had written you might have refused to see me. My timing on the previous occasion was unforgivably clumsy—I apologise for that. To expect you to reach a decision at this moment would be just as unreasonable, so with your permission I will call on you tomorrow afternoon—shall we say at three o'clock?'

'All right, Philippe.'

'Then let us rejoin your parents.'

On the drive home Mrs Robinson was full of excited comment about the charm of Philippe. 'I can't think why you didn't tell us more about him,' she said.

Rose knew there would be no escape from their interested, loving curiosity until she told them the truth.

'He asked me to marry him,' she said. 'But I—well, I wasn't sure. That was really why I came home.'

'Quite right too,' approved her father. 'It's a big decision to get married and you're very young—you want to make sure you'd be doing the right thing. I must say he seemed to me a really nice young man, though.'

'Charming, absolutely charming,' agreed her mother. 'And lives in a château, you say?'

Rose nodded. 'I showed you the pictures.'

'Be a nice place to come and stay with you,' remarked her father. 'But of course, it's your decision. This is something on which you must make up your own mind.'

'Of course, if you don't love him—' began Mrs Robinson.

'But I do.'

The words burst from Rose's heart. She surprised herself with the vehemence of her tone. Mr and Mrs Robinson glanced at each other.

'Then what is it that's worrying you, dear? I mean, there's no hurry about it, you could get engaged and marry next year, perhaps.'

'I—I'm just not sure.'

'You're quite right to take your time. But he's obviously deeply devoted to you. I mean, coming all this way and taking us all out—he'd no need to do that.'

In the comfort and security of her own home it was possible to believe that marriage with Philippe would work. Besides, since she had been away from him, away from the Château and Chandelle, she had been forced to acknowledge that a part of her heart lay there for ever. She had felt depressed since she returned home, those terrible mundane jobs she had applied for awoke no enthusiasm in her—she had been so very much happier helping Miss Grantchester than she possibly could be working as a snack bar attendant or dental receptionist, let alone as a canvasser for those bits of plastic rubbish.

By the time Philippe was due to arrive the following afternoon Rose was still unsure what she would say to him. Her father was, of course, at school and her mother had gone, as was always her custom on the last Thursday of every month, to the Women's Institute meeting. Rose was alone in the house when Philippe rang the bell; she had been listening for it, though she made a pretence of reading a book.

She had rehearsed the scene in imagination, determined to greet him calmly, to sit opposite him in the same chair as she had done yesterday, to listen to all he had to say. But even when, with studied formality, she ushered him into the room, she still had no idea what she should answer. Could she bear to tell him to leave so that never again would she stand close to him as she did now, with her heart beating so fast and with that exquisite feeling of being so very much alive and alert? Why should the very presence of this man in the same room as her give that startling brilliance to everything, make every remark seem more telling, every sense more vital?

'Won't you sit down, Philippe,' she invited him, gesturing towards the settee just as she had planned.

Philippe, however, had a different scenario in mind. He did not relinquish her hand after the formal greeting, but led her towards the settee with him, so that she had perforce to sit close beside him. Objectivity became a little less possible and the fact that he continued to hold her hand did nothing to help matters, especially when he lifted it and pressed his lips first against the back of her hand and then with a more sensual kiss, into her palm, looking up at her as he did so with a quizzical expression. Reason told her to pull her hand away, but reason was not the dominant faculty in her being just at that moment.

'Rose, I have come for my answer. Forget what happened that last evening at the Château—I know I frightened you. Let me ask you, now that you have had time to consider more rationally—will you marry me?'

She looked up at him then, looked deeply into those very dark brown eyes, and it seemed to her that his gaze was so penetrating he must be able to read from her face how deep was her longing for him. It had nothing to do with rational thought, though she knew that the reasons why she had refused him before were all as real and strong as ever, but there was only one answer she could give.

'Yes, Philippe, I'll marry you.'

A smile spread over his handsome face. He had triumphed, his pleasure showed in the warmth of his eyes and gently he leaned forward and kissed her on the lips. It was just a light kiss, no more—and almost immediately he straightened up.

'Thank you, Rose. And the next question is—when?'

'Perhaps—next spring?'

'Why do you wish to wait so long? Are you so fond of your English winters?'

'No, but—well, I—I thought five or six months would be a reasonable time for an engagement.'

'That reminds me—the engagement ring.' Philippe jumped to his feet. 'Come, let us go and buy one.'

With his usual sweeping enthusiasm, he

ushered her out to his car and drove to an exclusive jewellery shop. Rose was overwhelmed at the beauty of the ring, and horrified at the cost of it—a huge diamond surrounded by eight sapphires.

'I'll never dare to wear it,' she whispered.

'Nonsense. You'll soon come to take it for granted. I think it looks just as if it belongs there, on your finger. Shall we go back and break the news to your parents? And shall we tell them it's to be in a month's time?'

'So soon?'

'Why not? We have made up our minds—what is the point of waiting, Rose? I would not like to think of you taking one of those jobs you spoke of, just to pass the time away.'

Rose didn't like that idea either, and the thought of returning to Chandelle with Philippe was like a dream, so she allowed him to have his way. Mrs Robinson, who only yesterday had been advocating several months' engagement, was won over with surprising ease to the idea that Philippe insisted was so much more sensible, of having the wedding the following month. Rose's father said to count him out of it—he left such things to the womenfolk.

So a date was fixed and Philippe left soon afterwards, saying that this was an especially busy time of the year for him because of the grape harvest—he liked to keep an eye on things for himself. In fact it was unlikely that he would manage to get back to England until the eve of the wedding.

CHAPTER NINE

The knapped flint of the twelfth-century church gleamed in the autumn sun as Rose stepped out of the car, dressed in a simple, princess style white wedding gown. Her father took her arm and led her to the thatched porch where two cousins in pink, her bridesmaids, waited to follow her up the aisle. There was a momentary pause while they arranged themselves in order, then the notes of the bridal march boomed from the organ and the faces in the crowded church turned to catch their first glimpse of the bride.

Rose had wanted a quiet wedding, but despite her pleas, somehow it had grown, fed by Mrs Robinson's enthusiasm. Rose was her only daughter, she was marrying a handsome young man of wealth and position, so many friends and relations would be terribly disappointed if they missed such an occasion. Mrs Robinson had added and added to the list of invitations until there were about sixty people sitting expectantly on the left-hand side of the nave. The du Caines were thinly represented by comparison, but that was only to be expected when they lived in France. Philippe had a friend from his university days to act as best man, and there were a few board members from the London office, with their wives. Aunt Celia had been unable to travel. She had wanted to—the spirit was willing, but the flesh now too weak, she had written to Rose. Nevertheless she had wanted to know the exact time of the ceremony so that she could sit quietly and allow her imagination to be there with them.

Rose held her head high. The steadiness of her father's gait helped to control her nervousness, his arm was as firm as a rock and never had she been more grateful of its understanding strength than she was as she walked the length of the aisle towards

Philippe. He turned as the notes of the organ swelled through the church. Her face was covered by her veil, her eyes downcast as she took her place beside him and the vicar begun to intone the service. As though in a dream she made her vows and heard Philippe give his. A friend from her old school, a contralto with a beautiful voice, sang an aria; it was a delightful and very moving service.

Afterwards there was a lavish reception at a nearby country club. Her parents, though by no means rich, had over the years, saved money so that they could give financial help to Rose if she went to university, or if she needed it to set up home. Since her marriage to Philippe eliminated both those possibilities, Mrs Robinson had easily been able to persuade her husband that they should at least give her a really good wedding. Philippe must not think that he was marrying into an impoverished family, she said, drawing herself up with perky dignity.

Later in the afternoon Rose changed out of her wedding dress. She had complied with all the old traditional saying, wearing something old, something new, something borrowed and something blue. As she left with Philippe she turned and threw her bridal bouquet—it was caught by one of her cousins, who stood holding it starry-eyed. Then the car pulled away, they were heading for the airport and from there they would fly to Paris.

Philippe had arranged for a chauffeur-driven car to meet them on arrival at Orly Airport and take them straight to their hotel. Rose found it hard to believe she was not dreaming, that she was here in Paris again—that she was now Mrs—or Madame—du Caine, Philippe's wife. The thought made her shy of him and to counteract this she looked brightly about her as they drove along the boulevards into the great city and crossed the Seine, then turned along the Champs-Elysées towards the famous Arc de Triomphe.

It was close on eight o'clock when they were ushered to their suite in the hotel, one of the best in Paris. Rose felt a trifle overawed by such grandeur, though she tried not to show it.

'Shall I order dinner to be sent up here—or would you prefer to go down to the dining-room?' Philippe asked.

Her natural reserve and modesty made her feel it would be brazen to want to dine there alone with him, in the intimacy of their own rooms. She could not quite bring herself to state such a preference.

'I think we should go down,' she replied, with what she hoped was sophisticated nonchalance.

Philippe raised one mocking eyebrow and nodded his acceptance of her decision.

'Downstairs it is, then. Ten minutes to freshen up, shall we say? I'll phone down and reserve a table.'

Rose had no need to do more than wash and run a comb through her hair, her skin still had the bloom of the summer's tan and she wore only a little light make-up.

'Ready,' she said brightly.

'Good girl! Come on, let's go.'

Philippe was well known in the hotel, and the head waiter moved forward at once as they entered the spaciously plush dining-room.

'Good evening, Monsieur du Caine. This way, please.'

He led them to a table, discreetly placed in an alcove, held the chair for Rose and once they were seated, lit three candles in a silver candelabrum. A band played pleasant muted music; there were several other diners in the room and it seemed to Rose that curious glances were cast in their direction. She decided that it was Philippe who aroused this interest, he was so tall and handsome and with that arrogant bearing of his commanded attention wherever he went.

With all the excitement of the day Rose had eaten little and still did not feel hungry, but when the food came it looked so appetising, smelled so tempting and tasted so delicious that she surprised herself by eating well. Philippe ordered champagne, and she sipped it and enjoyed it, though she refused more than one glass. She began to feel dreamily relaxed and happy.

'Shall we dance?' Philippe suggested.

The floor was small, the band played a smoochy tune, and she was clasped close in his arms, swaying to the music. The way he held her, tenderly, possessively, produced a warm, cherished feeling that was wholly sweet. He smiled as she looked up at him, a smile that demanded a reciprocal smile from her, and there was a unity between them in that moment. Despite the throng of couples around them she felt alone with Philippe—and she knew that the rapt expression on his face was for her and her alone.

A flash of light made her blink. Someone was taking photographs. She glanced towards it and immediately more flashes lit the darkened scene. Philippe swore angrily. The head waiter hurried forward and peremptorily ordered the photographers from the restaurant. He was most apologetic, he could not think how they had managed to get in, he ought to have taken special care, especially as Monsieur was there with his beautiful young bride—

'Send coffee and cognac up to my suite,' Philippe ordered. 'Come, Rose.'

In the lift he relaxed a little.

'I should have warned you. That's one thing you'll have to get used to, I'm afraid—publicity. I don't mind it in its right place, of course, but they will persist in pushing one's private life into the limelight.'

'But who could have told them?' Rose asked. 'I mean, there was only the local reporter at our wedding.'

'That would be enough if it was passed on to the right papers. Besides, several people in the restaurant recognised me, that was quite obvious. The waiter himself might have rung the press, if they made it worth his while.'

'I'm sorry, Philippe.'

'Good heavens, it's not your fault.'

'You should have explained why you wanted to dine in our room,' she told him.

'Ah, but that was not really the reason.'

They walked across the thickly carpeted corridor, paused while he put the key in the lock. A few minutes later a waiter appeared with a trolley on which was coffee, cognac and a dish of after-dinner mints. Rose sat down to drink her coffee, but Philippe remained standing. He wandered around the room, restlessly as if he had far too much energy to sit, he was in no mood to relax. He switched on some music and moved towards her chair, holding out his hand.

'Shall we finish that dance?'

She was in his arms again and this time in very truth they were alone. There was no one to watch, no photographers to flash their lights as he held her close and lowered his cheek till it was pressed caressingly against hers. He placed both her hands so that they were resting on his shoulders and with her fingers she touched his neck, just where those tight black curls sprang above his jacket collar.

Philippe swayed to the dance music, though his hands were now stroking her back, straying down just beyond the small of her back, holding her so close she could feel the strength of his body against hers, as if he would mould her pliant softness to his shape. With experienced hands he unfastened the long back zip of her dress; she had scarcely realised it, but the dance had carried them towards the open door of the bedroom.

He kissed her, a long, lingering unhurried kiss that blended their lips and carried his passion through her mouth, so that her response was inflamed in tune with his. Tenderly he eased her dress from her shoulders, and it dropped to the floor. He kissed her again and as he did so his hands reached behind her to unfasten her tiny, frilly bra. Unresisting, she allowed him to remove it, to drop it beside the dress, then he stepped back, still holding her hands, looking at her, and because of the pleasure and excitement that lit his face, she felt no embarrassment. She was his wife—her body was his, her life in future would be forever linked to his.

'How beautiful you are, Rose. Beautiful
—beautiful!'

Because he said it with so much meaning
and because his face, his deep, dark brown
eyes, his mouth, sensual from kissing her,
were living proof of the strength of his
desire, she felt beautiful. She felt her
breasts swell in response to his gaze, the
nipples seeming to stand proud, and a
yearning for him ran down through her
narrow waist, made a hollow in her flat
stomach. Then once again she was in his
arms, she was swung up off her feet as if
she had been no more than a child and
carried towards the big bridal bed...

The telephone shrilled, but Philippe
ignored it. He placed Rose down, but
the phone rang again and again. It was
going to be persistent.

'Excuse me,' he said, then with a smile.
'Don't go away.' He lifted the receiver.
'Hello.'

His voice was anything but friendly and
Rose felt sorry for whoever was at the other
end of the line. She expected him to deal
with the caller brusquely and hang up, but
he held on to the line and she saw his
expression change to a look of seriousness.

'I see. Yes—has everything been done that can be done? She's still unconscious—I see. Yes.'

He listened again. Rose sat up on the bed, pulling a coverlet over her nakedness. She felt frightened, though she did not know why. Philippe's face seemed to drain of colour, his vitality did not diminish, but somehow it lost its glow. She had no contact with him now—if they had been more companionable she might have reached out her hand and taken hold of his in instinctive comfort, but she did not know him well enough to do that. He had moved a mile away from her, though he stood still within an arm's length.

'Yes, of course, I'll come at once.'

He hung up the receiver and turned to Rose. She was a cocoon of counterpane, with her knees clasped close to her chest, a pyramid shape, hidden from him except for her small face and fair wavy hair.

'It's Aunt Celia,' he explained. 'She's had a fall—down the steps, missed her footing somehow. She's unconscious—they don't know yet how bad it is.'

'Oh, Philippe! I'm so sorry—'

'Get dressed. Ring that bell for a maid

to help you to pack. I'll phone and charter a plane.'

He lifted the telephone again even as he spoke. Rose tossed aside the coverlet and did as he asked. She picked up the bra and the dress that lay where they had fallen.

'The plane will be ready as soon as we get to the airport.'

He lifted the phone again and ordered a taxi. The maid was clearly surprised to be called back to pack when she had hung up their things only such a short time before, but when she understood the urgency she set to with a will. In no time they were away from the hotel, driving through the gaily lit streets back to Orly.

'I'm sorry, Rose,' said Philippe. 'We'll come back to Paris for a few days as soon—'

'Don't worry about that,' Rose interrupted him. 'I'm almost as worried as you are about Miss Grantchester. Don't forget I grew very fond of her while I was at the Château.'

'She has seemed almost indestructible—I often forget how old she is.' He sounded as if he blamed himself in some way for the accident.

'That was the way she liked it,' Rose

reminded him. 'It was the same with her blindness. She made so little of it you could easily believe she could see a lot better than she does.'

'I owe her such a lot,' Philippe murmured. 'I have so little real family. There's only Aunt Celia and—'

He stopped. Rose hoped he was going to turn towards her and add 'and now you', but he didn't. He seemed almost to have forgotten she was beside him. He was thinking of someone else, and Rose felt saddened that there was so little she could do to comfort him. He scarcely seemed to be the same man who had been holding her in his arms with such racing passion such a short time ago.

The flight was quick. A car waited to take them the last few miles to the Château, and it was only a little past midnight when they arrived. It had been inadvisable to move Aunt Celia, instead a day and a night nurse had been engaged. The doctor came forward to greet them, his manner, calm though grave, designed to reassure.

'How is she?' Philippe asked anxiously.

'Holding her own,' the doctor said. 'Amazing woman. Her constitution is extraordinarily robust for her age, it's a miracle that with a fall like that there were no bones broken.'

'Do you think she'll be all right?'

'Difficult to be sure at this stage—that was why I felt you should be sent for, though naturally we were sorry to disturb you at the very beginning of your honeymoon.'

Philippe brushed the doctor's apology aside.

'May I see her?'

'Indeed you may. She is still unconscious. I should be happier if she showed some sign of coming round, and it may be that the sound of your voice will get through to her.'

'I'll go to her at once.'

Rose followed as Philippe took the stairs two at a time. At the door of Aunt Celia's room he hesitated momentarily, then straightened his shoulders and quietly opened the door. He moved to the bedside, while Rose stopped by the shining barley-sugar twisted rail at the foot of the old-fashioned brass half-tester. Miss Grantchester's face looked pinched and colourless against the snowy pillow. With gentle fingers Philippe lifted a lock of hair that lay across her cheek, moving with the regular rhythm of her breathing.

'Aunt Celia,' he murmured. 'Aunt Celia, this is Philippe. Can you hear me?'

There was no response.

'Try again,' urged the doctor. 'You too, madame—you speak to her.'

Rose started at the unfamiliar mode of address.

'Miss Grantchester—Aunt Celia—may I call you that now I'm one of the family?'

Philippe spoke a little louder. 'Aunt Celia, I've brought Rose back to you. You remember—you wanted me to marry Rose, didn't you?'

There was a slight flicker of her eyelids. The doctor held the old lady's wrist, taking her pulse. There was a scurry of paws on the other side of the bed, and Gigi raised herself, pushing her cold damp nose under the mistress's hand.

'Who let that dog in?' demanded the nurse. 'We can't have it here in a sickroom.'

'Gigi's her guide dog, perhaps you didn't realise that? They are never separated.'

'Leave the dog for now,' ordered the doctor.

As Gigi licked Miss Grantchester's hand

and Philippe spoke again, the tired old eyes flickered once more. She was regaining consciousness. For just a few brief moments she seemed to be aware of them gathered around her bed.

'Philippe,' she whispered.

He was holding her hand with a reassuring pressure. Rose moved across to stand beside him and the old lady's eyes seemed to flicker across to her, giving the uncanny feeling that she could see.

'Hello, Aunt Celia—it's me, Rose.'

'Rose.'

She repeated the name, and a slight smile lighted her pallid face. She seemed to be reaching out her other hand, groping, and Rose leaned over to grip it. The effort seemed too much and almost immediately Aunt Celia had sunk back deep into the pillow. Rose looked at the doctor in alarm, but he was nodding with every appearance of satisfaction. He beckoned them to follow him out of the room. Philippe dragged the reluctant Gigi out too, as the nurse began to bustle about officiously.

'I think we can feel guardedly hopeful, now that she has regained consciousness,' the doctor said. 'She is sleeping more normally now—it is still touch and go, of course, at her age—but there's plenty of fight left in her. I wouldn't be at all surprised if she pulled through. Remarkable woman—remarkable!'

'She certainly is,' Philippe agreed. 'Will you take a drop of something before you leave, doctor?'

'A small cognac would be most welcome. But don't let me keep you young people up—Madame du Caine looks quite worn out.'

'I—I'm all right,' Rose protested.

Philippe, for the first time in several hours, looked at her.

'What a day it's been for you, Rose! You get along to bed—'

'Well, if there's nothing I can do?'

She really was tired, now she stopped to think about it. While there had been so much involvement she had been able to keep going, now all they could do was to wait and hope and pray.

'Not a thing. Off you go.'

'Goodnight, Doctor.'

'Goodnight, *madame*.'

Rose did not say goodnight to Philippe. No doubt he would come up to share the big bed with her when he had taken that drink with the doctor and seen him out of the house. She left the door unlocked—no need any more to worry about placing a chair against the handle of the communicating door either. Her suitcase had been placed in the room and her nightie taken out and was lying on the turned-down sheets ready for her. She changed quickly and snuggled down thankfully and almost immediately the events of the day were blotted out in sleep.

The new day dawned and brightened with ever-increasing hope. Rose slept late and undisturbed. She slipped out of bed and padded across the room and cautiously opened the door to Philippe's room. His bed was still turned down for the night and his pyjamas lay folded in place. Rose rang the bell for Murielle, who came in with her usual beaming smile.

'Mademoiselle Celia is a little better this morning—isn't it wonderful, *madame*?'

'It most certainly is.'

Murielle nodded emphatically. 'The doctor is with her now. But I heard him tell Monsieur Philippe that he was more than satisfied with her progress. Shall I fetch your breakfast, *madame*?'

'I could have it downstairs, if that would

be less trouble. You must all be very busy.'

'It's no trouble, *madame*. In fact I believe the maids have already cleared the breakfast-room. I'll fetch it straight away.'

As the morning wore on Rose was a little dispirited that there was nothing she could do to help. Philippe, she was told, had stayed up all night, by his aunt's bedside. He had been there when she wakened again and they had spoken a few words together. The doctor had confirmed that Mademoiselle Grantchester seemed set to recover. The sadness that had hung over the Château lifted as the cheery bustle of the day continued.

Philippe went out to check over some problems on the estate. Rose did not see him till lunch time, and then it was easy to see that he could scarcely keep his eyes open. He came into the dining-room but did not take his place at the table.

'I think I'll lie down for an hour or so—if you'll excuse me,' he said.

'But of course! You must be worn out. Oh, Philippe, isn't it wonderful what progress Aunt Celia is making?'

'Yes. Her spirit is strong. She still feels she has much to live for, and that is all-important at her age. Have you seen her today, Rose?'

'Only briefly. They said she had to rest and get her strength back, but perhaps I can sit beside her a little while this afternoon.'

'Yes, do that.'

He swayed slightly, and Rose could see the fatigue on his face. 'Off you go and lie down. I'll see that you're called at once if there's any development,' she commanded.

Without further ado he obeyed. Rose ate her lunch alone. She did not mind that at all, her sympathy and understanding overflowed towards Philippe. How long he slept she had no idea. When she went to her room to change before dinner the bed in his room was rumpled and empty. Quietly she prepared to join him downstairs, but when she entered the drawing-room it was quite empty. She rang the bell and a manservant entered. She had seen him before, but did not know him as she did Yvette or Murielle.

'You rang, *madame*?'

'Er—I was wondering—do you know where my husband is?'

'Monsieur Philippe?' The raised eyebrows suggested that she should not be asking him that. 'I understand Monsieur went into Les Virages, *madame*. He left instructions that he would not be back to dinner.'

'Oh.'

'The meal is ready, *madame*. Shall I serve it now?'

Rose hoped her disappointment, her dismay did not show on her face. 'Yes, please.'

For the third time that day Rose found herself eating alone, and a deep anger and resentment grew. The food seemed to her tasteless and she ate little of it, her mind and emotions in a turmoil. How could Philippe go off to Les Virages today of all days! She was his wife now, how dared he rush so uncaringly to the arms of that other girl—one of his mistresses, she remembered Kerry had laughingly described her. Admittedly there had been no sign of any other woman than the lovely brunette she had seen in his car that day in Les Virages—but that was one too many, as far as Rose was concerned.

As anger and resentment boiled up inside her she knew she could not bear him to touch her. He could not just come back and expect to share her bed—somehow she must take some steps to prevent that; she would have to push the chair against the door again. But would that keep him out now? Surely there must be a key somewhere? Then it occurred to her that now she was in a very different position than before—she was mistress of the household, it would seem perfectly normal for her to take over her duties immediately. As a first step she demanded that the keys of all the rooms be brought to her and particularly all the spare keys.

If the servants thought such a request odd they were too well trained to display their curiosity. The keys were placed in Rose's bedroom, just as she commanded, and as soon as she was alone she sorted through them. There were three large bunches of keys tied together with string and in addition a box of assorted spare keys. It seemed that generally little attention was paid to locking doors in the Château and odd keys must have been gathered together over the years. Some were so large that it was obvious they would not fit, others of a different type and some so small they must have belonged to chests of drawers or bureaux rather than to doors.

One after the other she tried the keys on

the rings and at last found one that turned the lock. It was a little stiff from disuse, but by leaning her shoulder against the door it was possible to turn it. Triumphant, she unfastened the key from the others, then rang for Murielle to return the rest of the keys.

Philippe still had not returned. Rose enquired once more from the nurse about Aunt Celia and having made sure there was nothing she could do and that progress was being maintained, she announced her intention of going to bed.

She did not retire immediately but made her preparations and then put on a negligee, turned off the light and sat by the window, in that same chair where Philippe had once waited for her. It was barely ten o'clock when his car swung up the drive and halted outside. She looked down, unseen, as he stepped out. All signs of tiredness had left him, there was a spring in his gait as he mounted the steps; he seemed to be in excellent high spirits after his visit to Les Virages, Rose thought.

A few minutes later she heard him walk quietly along the corridor. He was calling in on Aunt Celia. There was a brief whispering conversation with the nurse, and

Rose waited breathless as she heard him retrace his steps to the door of her room. He tried the handle and found it locked. Presently there were sounds of movement from the adjoining room—and then she saw the knob of the communicating door open. There was a thud as he gave it a push.

'Rose?'

His voice sounded puzzled. She did not move. He rattled the door handle and called again. This time he raised his voice a little, then he knocked.

'Rose, open the door!'

A note of anger had crept into his voice. Still she made no reply. He tried two or three times more, then silence descended on the Château. Rose crept into bed and curled up miserably alone and cried herself to sleep.

CHAPTER TEN

A knocking on the door awakened her and she stirred, unrefreshed from her troubled sleep. Memories of last night rushed back. What time was it? Was Philippe—?

'*Madame,* are you awake?'

It was Murielle with the breakfast tray. Rose padded across the room and opened the door to her. The little maid seemed to give her an enquiring glance and Rose hoped she was not looking red-eyed from crying so much last night. She tried to brighten up and smile, but it was doubtful whether she really convinced Murielle that she was the happiest of young brides.

All Rose could think was that another day had begun, that her heart was full of resentment and sadness, that this would be the pattern of the days for the rest of her life. It was unbearable. She should never have entered this loveless marriage; the idea of a *mariage de convenance* had been repugnant from the first, but she had come to believe that because she loved Philippe she would be able to cope with it. It was not so—her deep love for him made it harder.

Philippe was out all day. Aunt Celia was getting strong remarkably quickly, soon they said she would be getting up for an hour or two, and Rose was allowed to spend rather more time with her. Her mind was as alert as it had been previously and she wanted Rose to tell her all about

241

the wedding, holding her hand in her thin dry fingers as she listened.

'You've made me so happy, my dear. Because I have you and Philippe, I feel I have so much to live for. He needed a wife, I've told him so many times in the past, but he always just shrugged it off.'

Rose felt more sad and empty than ever as she listened. She was sure now that Philippe had been pressurised into marrying her by Aunt Celia. No doubt he expected her to make a biddable, uncomplaining consort who would make no trouble about his continuing escapades with other women, but Rose could just not be complacent like that.

'The du Caines are a great family, Rose,' Aunt Celia rambled on. 'It was a terrible disappointment to me that Philippe was an only child. I hope you'll have lovely babies to waken up the old Château. It needs young blood in it.' She paused, then said, 'They wonder where I get my will to live—I'll tell you what I think. It's you who's given me hope, Rose. More than anything I want to hold your first child in my arms—yours and Philippe's.'

A smile lit her pale face, as if she could already imagine the tiny bundle that would carry the name of du Caine on into the next generation.

'Don't blush, my dear. I'm an old lady and I feel I can talk freely to you. I don't care whether it's a boy or a girl, at least I shall know the line will be carried on. I only hope you won't waste too much time—none of this modern nonsense of waiting two or three years, please—'

Her voice trailed off. Rose sat silent, her cheeks burning. It was impossible to answer, but she remained determined she would not be cajoled into a relationship that was now repugnant to her. Never! Never would she allow Philippe into her room. If he had expected that he could marry her and carry on just as he had done as a bachelor, going to visit that girl in Les Virages whenever he fancied, then he would have to change his mind. She would have walked out and returned to England, but it was unthinkable to leave because Aunt Celia was still so fragile, any additional upset might cause a relapse. She would bide her time until the right moment came.

She did not see Philippe until dinner that evening. It was an uncomfortable meal. They made cool polite conversation, like strangers in a restaurant, so that it seemed to Rose that Philippe felt no tension—he certainly showed no sign of emotion as the servants moved quietly about the room, discreetly waiting on them.

'I trust you have had a pleasant day, my dear?'

Was there a hint of sarcasm in the words? If so she ignored it.

'Pleasant enough, thank you, Philippe. And you?'

He seemed to be in an expansive mood, relaxed and smiling as if he did not care at all that she had locked her door against him the previous night. He told her something of the work he had been engaged in and as she forced herself to show interest he began to explain something of the process of wine-making and the care that had to be lavished on the vines, and he was so knowledgeable that she could not help being fascinated. They took coffee together in the drawing-room, but she refused his suggestion that she should take a liqueur.

'It would help you to relax,' Philippe suggested.

Still she shook her head. She had no wish to relax. He stood with a hand on the

244

bottle, looking down at her speculatively. It was the look that in the past had made her knees wobbly, that started the blood coursing in her veins, but she turned away and hardened her heart towards him. She was determined not to be beguiled into his arms. She finished her coffee and stood up resolutely.

'I think I'll have an early night. Goodnight, Philippe.'

Unsmiling he raised the brandy glass he was holding, bowed his head slightly, then strode across the room. For a moment Rose thought he was going to bar her exit, but with a mocking smile he opened the door for her. If she had been older and wiser she might have read in his expression that this was not to be the end of the matter. As it was she held her head high as she swept past him and climbed the stairs.

She locked the door as soon as she entered the room, then she glanced across at the communicating door and a gasp of dismay rose in her throat. The key was missing again. She ran across the room and turned the handle, and the door opened silently and easily. She searched the floor, under the nearby furniture, hoping against hope that the key had fallen from the lock. It was nowhere to be seen. It must have been removed deliberately, and there was only one person who could have taken it—Philippe.

What was more, the small chair that she had previously used to prop against the handle had also gone. There was nothing in the room that she could now use for such a purpose. Shakily she walked across to the chair by the window, on the opposite side of the room, and sat down. She sat there, staring blankly at the door. She could not have said how long she waited—perhaps half an hour, or an hour—time seemed almost to stand still.

As on the previous night she heard Philippe's footsteps moving along the corridor outside, making his last call to see that Aunt Celia was comfortable for the night, to have a word with the nurse. Tension increased in Rose as she listened for sounds of movement from his rooms. He took his time. Her nerves were almost at screaming point when at last she heard the light tap on the communicating door.

She made no reply. She curled herself even more tightly into the chair, with her legs tucked beneath her, her hands gripping the arms, her gaze fixed on the door handle. It turned silently. Slowly the door was pushed open. Philippe stood just inside the room. He wore a short bathrobe of dark material wrapped closely around him and tied at the waist with a cord.

'Rose.'

His voice was soft, little more than a whisper. He stayed silhouetted against the light from his room, adjusting his eyes to the darkness. Rose held her breath and remained motionless. Philippe moved forward a few steps, saw that the bed was empty, his head jerked suspiciously around and almost immediately he realised where she was.

'Rose?'

There was hesitation in his voice, but he began to walk towards her.

'What do you want?' She spoke at last.

'What do I want?' He gave a short mirthless laugh. 'Rose, you are my wife—surely you haven't forgotten?'

She shook her head dully. No, she had not forgotten—it was he who had been so easily able to forget. How could he expect her to react with enthusiasm to his approach now? He was so strong, his size and power had dominated the room the minute he entered it, she acknowledged that he could easily take her and she would be totally unable to defend herself. A passive resistance was all she could exert.

Cautiously he approached until he was standing immediately in front of her. She refused to look up at him. His hand rested on her head, moved in a caress down her cheek, but she jerked her face away from him.

'Look at me, Rose. Don't be frightened.'

His voice was still gentle. Then as she made no move to comply with his request his hand cupped more firmly beneath her chin, at first she continued to resist, but as the pressure of his fingers tightened she allowed him to lift her head.

In the moonlight she could see his face, read puzzlement and disbelief in his expression, felt the magnetism of those deep, dark eyes that regarded her so intently. She hardened her heart against their plea, and gave a short dry laugh; he was unused to being rejected where women were concerned.

'What game is this you're playing at?'

There was a flare of anger in his voice.

'It's no game, I assure you.'

'Rose, I must have an explanation. Why

did you lock your door last night?'

'I should have thought that was obvious. I didn't want to be disturbed.'

'And tonight, if I had not taken—precautions—?'

He put his hand into his pocket and lifted out the missing key. Her silence was answer in itself.

'When, may I ask, would you have deigned to be—er—disturbed?'

'Never—willingly.'

He drew in his breath sharply between his teeth. His hands dropped from her face to her shoulders and he grasped them hard, pulling her up so that she was forced to uncurl herself from the chair. She thought he was going to shake her, but instead he closed his arms around her as if he still expected to be able to caress her into compliance. She remained stiff and taut, resisting with every fibre of her being, with the full concentration of her mind. She would not allow herself to be won over by the powerful attraction of his physique.

'Am I to have no say in this sudden decision of yours?'

His voice held a note of studied persuasion. She struggled to free herself, and it was as if her movement triggered off an impulse that he had been holding in check, an impulse that was wholly male so that in preventing her escape from his arms they closed around her tightly, possessively.

Bodily he lifted her, with her arms pinioned at her sides, rendering her helpless, and carried her to the bed. He placed her on its softness without relinquishing his hold on her, so that he was lying on top of her. Rose felt the passion leap through his body—it could so easily have awakened an answering response in her own, but she lay tense and still. She closed her eyes. A tear rolled down her cheek—how different this was from her dream of making love with Philippe!

Suddenly his weight was lifted from above her. He released his hold and stood up. She became aware that her skirt had rucked up in the struggle and instinctively she reached down to tug it straighter over her thighs.

'Don't worry, Rose. If that is what you want, you can remain—*undisturbed*—for just as long as you wish.'

He took the key from his pocket and dropped it so that it fell into the neck of her blouse, just at the cleft between her breasts. Then he turned and strode back to his own room.

Slowly, shakily Rose rolled off the bed, undressed and changed into her nightie. She locked the door of the adjoining room, though now she knew she had no need to. Philippe would not come back. Victory was hers, but it left a very hollow feeling. It brought no joy, in fact she felt quite defeated. How long would she be able to maintain this dreary loveless life?

That was a question that dragged more and more depressingly into her spirits as the days passed. Though she tried to hide her dejection when she was with Aunt Celia, that astute old lady was not easily fooled. She instructed her to go out and walk in the gardens instead of sitting around indoors so much. Rose walked down to the villa, it was locked and empty, Kerry was still away. For the sake of the old lady Rose tried to snap out of the mood, but it was too deep-rooted for that; every day was just a dreary length of hours to be got through; the occasions she met Philippe for meals were tests of endurance, but she put on a pretence of brightness that she was far from feeling; the nights alone in the big double bed had a sadness that was the most unbearable of all.

Philippe worked hard; he was constantly busy, though he always spent some part of every day with Aunt Celia, he was away from home as much if not more than he had ever been. He at least had consolation—and since he did not love her, he was spared that special torture that Rose felt was hers alone. He had married her simply to be able to carry on his life style as before, so there was little for him to complain about in the present set-up, Rose decided.

The gloom in the Château was intensified when suddenly Aunt Celia took a turn for the worse. The steady improvement of the first week of her illness was reversed, for no apparent reason. It was not merely physically that she grew more ill, her temperature shot up in a way that caused the doctor to shake his head in alarm. The nurses hustled about with serious expressions on their faces, Rose spent more time than ever at Aunt Celia's bedside. She was there when the old lady started to talk deliriously, and there was one name she mentioned over and over again. Suzette.

'Philippe—Philippe, I—I want to see her.

Suzette. Philippe, bring—bring Suzette—'

Rose damped a cloth and soothed Aunt Celia's brow. She quietened down for a little time, then her hands, always so expressive, began to play with the coverlet again.

'Suzette—I—I should—see Suzette—'

She repeated the request so often that Rose and the nurse looked at each other and both knew that there was some meaning behind the words. Whatever the request, it came from a woman who was very, very ill and it had to be taken seriously. If there was anything that could be done to find this Suzette and bring her to Aunt Celia's bedside, then it must be done.

'All right. Lie quietly, Aunt Celia. I'll see Philippe and ask him to bring Suzette to see you.'

'Soon. I should have seen her before. I should—I—wicked old woman—'

'Shhh! It's all right, we'll find Suzette. Now you just rest.'

Rose hurried out of the room. She asked the servants and discovered that Philippe was in fact in his study at the Château that afternoon. She hurried to it and knocked on the door.

'Entrez.'

Philippe looked up as she went in, then rose to his feet. He waited for her to speak.

'It—it's Aunt Celia—'

He moved at once towards the door, obviously ready to rush up to the old lady.

'No, wait a minute. She's asking for someone—someone called Suzette. I—I thought you might know who it is.'

He looked at her with a stunned expression, as if scarcely able to believe her.

'Of course I know Suzette. Aunt Celia's always refused to meet her. I'll go up and find out what this is all about.'

Aunt Celia was resting when Philippe went into her room, Rose following anxiously. The nurse confirmed that Mademoiselle Grantchester had certainly been persistently asking to see someone called Suzette.

'Would it be possible for you to fetch the lady?' the nurse asked.

'Yes, of course. She lives in Les Virages. If you think it would be advisable, I'll go at once and fetch her.'

There was an eagerness in his step as he

strode from the room. Rose shrank back into a corner, her misery too intense to be hidden from her face, but Philippe never so much as glanced in her direction. The agony of that hour was something that Rose would remember for the rest of her life. She almost made up her mind to leave there and then, and was only prevented by her desire to know exactly who was this beautiful girl who had such a hold on Philippe that he had gone almost straight from the wedding ceremony to visit her.

So she kept a vigil by the window of her room, alone and sick at heart, until at last she saw Philippe's very dark blue car sweep into the drive. She caught a glimpse of the pale face, the bright dark hair, then the car slowed to a standstill almost immediately beneath her window so that the angle prevented her from seeing into it. Philippe's door opened, he got out and began to walk round the car. It was the moment Rose had been dreading, yet she was determined to face up to it with studied calm.

She turned away from the window, crossed the room and stepped out into the corridor. She moved quietly towards the stairs, deliberately keeping her movements unhurried, reminding herself that it was she who was mistress of the house, she who was Philippe's wife, whatever this other girl meant to him. But for Aunt Celia's illness she would never have countenanced this intrusion, now she was determined to face up to the challenge. Her pride must sustain her through the ordeal to come.

With one hand on the banister she began to descend the stair. She was perhaps halfway down when the manservant opened the double doors that led from the steps into the hallway. As he swung them wide Philippe entered—carrying the smiling girl in his arms. Rose stood stock still, shocked at such behaviour—he was actually carrying her over the threshold!

Then something about the girl's figure made Rose catch her breath. Those tiny legs, covered though they were in a pair of white slacks—surely there was something wrong with them? She noticed how light the girl was, how easily Philippe held her, yet how gently—and with a dismay that seemed to drain all the colour from her face, Rose realised that Suzette was crippled—badly crippled. The manservant brought in a folded wheelchair.

Philippe looked up and saw Rose

watching him with Suzette. He began to mount the stairs towards her, the weight of the small young lady negligible to him.

'Suzette, I'd like you to meet my wife. Rose, this is Suzette Montier.'

He still held Suzette in his arms, turning so that she could see Rose clearly and reach out one tiny pallid hand which Rose grasped in hers with willing sympathy.

'Madame du Caine, I am so pleased to meet you. You have a husband in a million! You do not know what a lucky young woman you are.'

Rose coloured, a deep searing shame rushing over her—she glanced at Philippe, but he began to move on upwards again. The servant had opened the wheelchair at the top of the stairs and Philippe placed Suzette in it. She gave a light laugh because she was a bit awkward at getting settled comfortably. Twisted though her poor body was, there was merriment and vivacity that gave a glow to her face. From the shoulders up Suzette was as lovely and normal as any other girl of her age, which Rose judged to be about twenty-five.

Philippe pushed the wheelchair along the corridor and into Aunt Celia's room. Rose followed, her emotions so mixed, feeling at such a loss to understand—it was all so different from what she had expected she just did not know how to react. She hesitated on the threshold and finally decided to wait outside the room. The door was left open and Philippe manoeuvred the wheelchair until Suzette was close enough to Aunt Celia's bed for them to clasp hands.

'*Bonjour,* Mademoiselle Grantchester.'

'My dear, can you forgive me for refusing to meet you before?' said Aunt Celia.

'But of course—there is nothing to forgive. I can understand how you felt, but all that is past now—'

Philippe turned, he saw Rose lingering on the threshold. He walked towards her and closed the door behind him, leaving his aunt and Suzette to talk together. He would have moved past Rose and continued towards the head of the stairs, but she put out a hand and touched his arm.

'Philippe,' she said, and all the trouble of her heart was in the word, 'who is Suzette?'

'I suppose you could call her a distant relation—on the wrong side of the sheet, as the saying goes. Perhaps I should have told you about her before, but it was not entirely my secret.'

'I—I would like to know, please, Philippe.'

He looked at her closely, as if aware of some subtle change in her that he could not account for.

'It's quite a long story. Let's go down to the terrace and have some tea.'

When they were settled together and the tea had been placed for Rose to pour and the servant had withdrawn so that they were alone, Philippe began to speak.

'You have seen Suzette—she's a marvellous person, she makes so little of her terrible affliction. When I first met her—it must be two or three years ago now, her mother was still alive. I belong to a group that raises money for charity and it was through them that I got to know her.'

He paused, deep in thought, remembering back.

'Gradually I discovered more about her. This is the part of the story that does not reflect well on my family. I hope you will not hold it against me, Rose—but I think it is right that you should know. I mentioned that Suzette is a distant relative—well, to put it bluntly, she is the illegitimate daughter of my grandfather.'

Rose's eyes opened wide. She was surprised, a little shocked, but she said nothing, waiting for him to continue.

'There is no doubt about it. Suzette was the product of an *affaire* he had with Mademoiselle Montier, very late in his life, after the death of my grandmother. I know I should not condone it, but I have come to understand. He must have been very lonely at that time and Mademoiselle Montier was, even when I met her so many years later, a warm-hearted and attractive woman. Evidently she was the consolation of my grandfather's later years, for he bought her a small house in Les Virages and she lived there for the rest of her life. Unfortunately when he died he made no other provision for her in his will. Suzette and her mother were in very straitened circumstances when I met them.'

He stood up and paced across the room, seeming to find it distressing to talk about it even yet.

'The house was totally unsuited to Suzette's condition and her mother was ill, dying in fact, though I did not know it at the time. It was a long time before I learned the truth of the story. Then it was only because, quite by chance, I came across some old papers of my grandfather's. Among them was a deed relating to the purchase of that little house in Les Virages, and it was then I began to put two and two together. When I first questioned her, Mademoiselle Montier was reluctant to tell me the full story. She said the old man had been very good and kind to her, she had no wish to distress his family and Suzette had no idea who her father was.

'I felt obligated to help them even more than I had done, and I wished to arrange for them to move into a bungalow where Suzette could get about in her wheelchair. I felt that we owed it to Suzette to acknowledge her—but Aunt Celia was horrified at the very thought. She felt the *affaire* besmirched the family honour, and though she agreed willingly enough to my spending as much money as was necessary to improve their circumstances, she quite set her heart against meeting Suzette. That was why I was so surprised when you told me today that Aunt Celia had asked to see her.'

Rose felt stunned and ashamed to think she had misjudged those frequent visits that Philippe made to Les Virages.

'Why didn't you tell me before, Philippe?' she asked.

He shrugged. 'It wasn't entirely my secret—Aunt Celia had made me promise not to mention it to a soul. No doubt I would have told you nevertheless, but—well, circumstances were never right.'

No, thought Rose—and that was because of my jealousy.

'I—I suppose, in a way, it was all due to that—that *mariage de convenance,*' she said.

'No, I don't think that's an entirely fair conclusion,' Philippe said. 'After all, the *affaire* did not take place until after my grandmother's death. I think I told you that I believe they were totally suited to each other and that it was a very successful and happy marriage despite its lack of love in the beginning.'

'You mean that love can grow—even if it's not there at the start?'

'I sincerely hope so, Rose.'

His voice was soft and gentle; she hoped and hoped that he might be right. If it was not too late, if she had not hurt him irreparably, she would try to be more lovable to him—then perhaps, in time...
There was a discreet cough and one of

262

the servants came out to the terrace.

'Excuse me, *monsieur,* the nurse says Mademoiselle Celia must rest now.'

Philippe was on his feet immediately.

'Order some fresh tea, Rose. I'll bring Suzette down.'

They sat together for a time on the terrace and then Rose pushed Suzette around the gardens in her wheelchair, while Philippe attended to his unfinished business in the study. She stayed on to dinner too, and it warmed Rose's heart to hear from Suzette just how much Philippe had done for her—not only had he provided everything she needed that money could buy, but he also gave so freely of his time, and for a man who was so busy, that showed a true spirit of friendship and generosity.

Suzette was delighted with the whole visit. Aunt Celia had wanted to make amends for her past rejection of Suzette by trying to persuade her to move into the Château, but Suzette had refused because she was so comfortable and happy in her little bungalow. Philippe had had it adapted so that she could manage everything for herself and had even provided her with a small motorised carriage, so her life was as comfortable as it could possibly be. She was happy to make the acquaintance of Aunt Celia, but she had no intention of making her connection with the family public knowledge, in fact she said she preferred the secret to remain within the family, for she felt that it could besmirch not only the name of Philippe's grandfather, but also that of her own dearly loved mother.

One thing was certain; Suzette enjoyed her first visit to the Château very much indeed and they all agreed that it should be repeated from time to time. The meeting had also been helpful to Aunt Celia; it was as if a weight had been lifted from her mind, and the nurse said she was sleeping naturally that evening and was confident that her health would go on improving.

It was late when Philippe carried Suzette out to his car and drove her away to Les Virages. Rose went slowly up to her own room. She knew it would be some time before Philippe returned, but she unlocked the communicating door and left it standing ajar. She undressed and got into bed, leaving the light on, taking a book in her hands, though she found it impossible to concentrate on it.

She heard the car return. It seemed ages before his footsteps came along the corridor outside her room. She was still uncertain what his reaction would be to that open door, shy of the invitation it represented. She heard the door of Philippe's room open and close—there was a long hiatus and then he stood there, still wearing the lightweight suit that he had changed into for dinner.

'Rose?'

She turned towards him, sitting up in the big bed.

'Yes, Philippe?' she replied.

She tried to make her voice sound normal, to conceal the emotions that were so strong they almost choked her. In two strides he was across by the bedside. He sat down and took her hands in his, looking deeply into her face, seeming unable to believe what he saw there.

Rose knew she ought to give him some explanation of her change of attitude—but how could she without hurting him, perhaps irreparably? Impossible to tell him that she had suspected him of having an affair with Suzette, of being disloyal to her immediately after their marriage. This afternoon she had learned so much more about this wonderful man that she had married—even if he did not love her, her feelings for him must be strong enough for their union to succeed. There was, however, one thing that really must be said. It took an effort, but Rose was determined not to shirk it.

'I—I've been troubled—about this *mariage de convenance*—but I believe you're right. I think perhaps that love will grow—' She had avoided looking at him as she spoke, but now she lifted her eyes to his face and gazed earnestly at him, long and steadily, before she finished. 'And—and I do so hope it will, because I love you so truly—'

She broke off. She had intended to say more, but it was impossible because she was clasped so tightly in Philippe's arms and he kissed and kissed her as if he would never stop. When at last he did, his voice was heavy with emotion.

'My darling, darling Rose, surely you must know how much I love you? Why on earth do you think I married you?'

'I—I thought—'

'I don't care what you thought. I've been so desperately in love with you from the start, only I was so afraid I would lose you. You're so young and sweet and innocent—I didn't want to rush you, but when that boy-friend of yours turned up, I was just so damned jealous I knew I had to ask you to marry me. I nearly went out of my mind when you refused and, what was worse, ran back to England with him.'

'But—but you always said you believed that a *mariage de convenance* was best—'

'I may have believed that once, but that was before I met you, Rose. You have changed my whole life. The trouble was I just didn't know how to get you to love me. You've been so remote, any time I tried to get near you, you seemed to reject me.'

'I'm sorry, Philippe, my darling. I—I just didn't understand—there've been so many things I haven't really understood. I'm sometimes a very silly girl—'

'Nonsense!'

He silenced her again with kisses, and from that night Rose came to know more positively than ever what a wonderful man she had married.

Early in the following year Kerry's baby girl was born, and that summer Rose had a son. Aunt Celia was delighted when she held him in her arms—she had quite regained her old strength and the nurses had long since left the Château. Outside the vines were ripening once again in the hot sun. The cycle of life went on and Rose was deeply content, knowing herself to be enmeshed at the centre of it, glowing in the constant love that Philippe lavished upon her.

The publishers hope that this book has given you enjoyable reading. Large Print Books are especially designed to be as easy to see and hold as possible. If you wish a complete list of our books, please ask at your local library or write directly to: Magna Large Print Books, Long Preston, North Yorkshire, BD23 4ND, England.

This Large Print Book for the Partially sighted, who cannot read normal print, is published under the auspices of

THE ULVERSCROFT FOUNDATION

THE ULVERSCROFT FOUNDATION

. . . we hope that you have enjoyed this Large Print Book. Please think for a moment about those people who have worse eyesight problems than you . . . and are unable to even read or enjoy Large Print, without great difficulty.

You can help them by sending a donation, large or small to:

**The Ulverscroft Foundation,
1, The Green, Bradgate Road,
Anstey, Leicestershire, LE7 7FU,
England.**
or request a copy of our brochure for more details.

The Foundation will use all your help to assist those people who are handicapped by various sight problems and need special attention.

Thank you very much for your help.